THE WHEELMAN

How the Slave Robert Smalls Stole a Warship and Became King

a novel by

Marshall Evans

Printed in the United States of America
First Printing, 2015

ISBN 978-0-9970127-0-5

Land's Ford Publishing
Spartanburg, SC, USA

Cover design by Fayssoux Evans
Cover photo from U.S. Library of Congress- Brady Collection

This is a novel. I made it up. All characters, except the historical ones, are fictional. Any resemblance to real persons, living or dead, is purely coincidental and unintentional. I didn't make up the historical events in this novel, although other people may have made them up earlier. Every word attributed here to Robert Smalls comes from published, primary sources of stellar reputation.

Parts of this book are written in Gullah, a creole language heard on the coast of South Carolina and Georgia. Wikipedia says some 250,000 people speak Gullah today, although an anonymous Wikipedia editor says a citation is needed to support this claim. Whatever the actual number of living speakers, the author of this book could not be counted among them. Fluent Gullah is largely beyond comprehension to most English speakers. It is, to the receptive ear, a magical language.

"But what about you?" he asked. "Who do you say I am?"- *gospel according to Matthew, Mark, and Luke, but not John.*

I have sailed the seas and come To the holy city – *W.B. Yeats*

The Hopeful

Two African-Americans were strolling in Beaufort, South Carolina in the 1870's. As their conversation bloomed, one declared Robert Smalls was a great man. In fact, he said, Robert Smalls was so great, he was probably the greatest man who ever lived on Earth.

This brought silence.

"But what about Jesus Christ?" his companion replied.

"Well," the original speaker said, "Robert Smalls is still young."

- Gullah folklore repeated in most historical accounts of Robert Smalls's life.

Uncle Romulus

On St. Simon's Island's western shore, Dunbar Creek winds to a place on the charts called Ebo Landing. Dunbar Creek is four- to six-feet deep and fifty-yards wide. It twists and turns for two and a half miles before it gets to Ebo Landing. Dunbar Creek is so narrow, and so long, and so twisty, I don't see how you could sail a small boat up it. I doubt sailing ships would ever have navigated it- even small coastal schooners. There are six or seven other spots on St. Simon's Island where deep, wide water runs right up to shore. Surely any sailing ship calling on St. Simon's- taking off cotton, delivering manufactured goods and slaves- would have gone to one of those other landings. I can't really see why a coastal schooner would find its way all the way up Dunbar Creek to Ebo Landing. But I'm thinking about it in a way that doesn't fit the stories. Maybe that doesn't make sense.

Gullah folklore has many stories. One of them tells of Sea Island slaves recently arrived from Africa. In this story the Africans could speak no English. They were sent to the fields, and when they refused to work, an overseer beat them. So the Africans turned themselves into birds and flew away to Africa.

The story has variations. Interviews with Gullah speakers compiled by a Federal Writers' Project during the Great Depression tell the story in some twenty different forms. In more recent times, the story found its way into print in numerous books, notably Toni Morrison's novel *Song of Solomon*. In the various tellings, the Africans include or don't include a pregnant woman with a nursing baby. The white overseer who beat the Africans is generally portrayed, somewhat sympathetically, as simply doing his job. The Africans are generally described as being unsuited to the work expected of them. The African language they speak is depicted sometimes as the quacking of marsh birds, sometimes as magical words that enable the slaves to take flight.

The events are often, but not always, said to have taken place within living memory. In these cases, the teller insists he heard the tale first-hand from so-and-so on a nearby plantation, who in his youth witnessed the metamorphosis and flight of the Africans with his own eyes. (These versions were recorded in a time when elderly storytellers would have known people who had been slaves.)

The location of the miracle is reported up and down the coast of Georgia and South Carolina, along the entire geographical range of Gullah culture. The settings may be inconsistent, but they are usually quite specific. Sometimes the story takes place at Ebo Landing on St. Simon's. Sometimes it is set on John's Island near Charleston, a hundred miles to the north. Other times the actual plantation name is given (Walburg's, for example, on St. Catherine's Island in Georgia.)

These stories are enchanting, entertaining, even inspiring, but entirely unsatisfactory to the modern mind. We want an objective, historical source. Fortunately, modern minds have found such a source in an 1802 slave rebellion at Ebo Landing on St. Simon's. That version of the story relies on a single account written by a plantation overseer. The overseer's letter tells of a small group of Igbo warriors who came on a slave ship from Africa to Savannah. There a St. Simon's plantation owner bought them and loaded them on a coasting schooner for delivery to their final destination.

En route, the slaves revolted, took control of the schooner, killed its crew, and dumped the bodies into the water. The slaves then landed along Dunbar Creek and fought some skirmishes on St. Simon's Island. According to the sole written source, after the local militia overwhelmed them, the Africans ran back into the marsh where they had come ashore- at Ebo Landing- and committed suicide by drowning themselves. ("Ebo" is a common variation of "Igbo.")

Gullah tradition also includes very different tales of African slaves who tried to walk back to their homeland on the water and drowned. This vein of storytelling provides a convenient link between the written record of the Ebo Landing rebellion and the flying bird stories. The whole genre is now generally lumped together as a variation on one event, reported at least once from a European perspective by the St. Simon's overseer. That makes the entire story cluster more approachable for Americans, who are are so terrified of the African roots of our culture.

In another branch of Gullah tradition, the ghosts of the Igbo who drowned themselves in Dunbar Creek are still there haunting the place. Local tradition forbids fishing in that spot, for fear of disturbing the Igbo. In the Gullah universe, the African ghosts still range over that creek and marsh in the nighttime.

Dunbar Creek empties into the Frederica River, which parallels the Intracoastal Waterway for much of St. Simon's Island's length. In fact, if your boat has a modest draft, you can take the entire Frederica River as a scenic detour off the Waterway, coasting by the ruins of the 18th-Century British fort, and then past Ebo Landing itself, only a a couple of miles to the south. The Frederica River provides convenient, protected anchorage for boaters transiting the Waterway.

About four years ago, I found myself spending the night anchored in the marsh within sight of Ebo Landing. My daughter Mary and I had left Charleston two nights before, sailing south toward the Bahamas. The boat was an old Pearson Vanguard, a 1960's vintage, thirty-two-foot sloop. I had found it for sale at a boatyard near Morehead City the previous fall, a couple of weeks after Grace died. A couple of years after the Great Recession had broken my business and bankrupted me. Nine months after a near-suicide had earned me a stay in a mental hospital.

My wife had agreed to let me offer two thousand dollars for the boat, two thousand dollars I had scrimped in my sock drawer in the months after the bankruptcy. She was thinking, she later admitted, that nobody would ever accept two thousand dollars for a sailboat that size. She had sense enough to know this kind of thing just wasn't done in the circumstances. I did not. I was too broken.

It was the Great Recession, and nobody was buying boats. This particular boat was decrepit. No one else wanted it. Three months after the owner rejected my original offer, he called me and gave in. So I emptied the sock drawer envelope, drove to North Carolina, and bought a forty-year-old boat with peeling paint, smelly cushions, and a rusty engine. The Pearson was well-built, though. With many, hard weekends of work, sanding and scraping and painting and filtering old diesel fuel, I had gotten it back in the water. Now we were sailing it to the Bahamas.

By that time, I had also, through what I can only account for as the grace of God, landed a job teaching English at the local community college. I had three months off for the summer. I talked Mary into coming along as crew.

We left Charleston harbor in the dark, motoring past Fort Sumter at sunset and through the jetties as night fell completely. We dodged a large inbound freighter towering black above us in the channel. Mary was terrified. I was terrified and trying not to let it show. I had been terrified and broken for at least two years. Losing Grace had devastated us both.

I took the first watch that night, setting sail in a gentle southeasterly breeze off Morris Island as Mary dozed below. The stars were brilliant in the May sky. The Milky Way rose and glistened from horizon to horizon.

After four hours, when I woke Mary for her first night watch ever, I could tell she was still scared. I pointed out the stars and the Milky Way. "Have you ever seen a night sky like that, ever in your life?" I asked. During my watch, a sentence from *Ulysses* had been running in my thoughts:

"The heaventree of stars hung with humid, night-blue fruit."

I said it out loud to Mary before I left her, but she was unimpressed.

Grace would have been transported. Grace found the wonder in art. She often rushed to me after she had read a great book or toured a new art museum, gushing with enthusiasm. After her trip to Europe, she remembered the most delightful details from great paintings, details I had remembered myself since my youth. It was our thing, the thing we liked to talk about, that nobody else in the family paid any attention to.

I left Mary in the cockpit and went below to toss and turn, sleeplessly, for the next four hours. When I came back on deck for my next watch, the stars were gone, and we were sailing in a dense fog.

Mary said she had given up looking out for ships and other boats. She had spent the last hour down below, staring at the radar screen, she said. The fog was too thick, the night too black, to see anything outside.

Well, that was no radar screen. That was an outdated laptop computer I had bought on Craigslist and loaded with free nautical charts. It showed our position off the coast, but it offered no indication whatsoever of other boats or ships passing by. For the past hour or more, we had been sailing at six knots through the fog with no lookout.

My anxiety mounted. It only mounted. It never dissipated on that trip.

By noon the next day, the fog lifted to become a haze with a mile or so of visibility, and we were off Savannah. But the wind had stopped. So we diverted from our offshore course, motored into St. Catherine's Sound on the Georgia coast, and spent the night anchored in Walburg's Creek, alongside what had once been Walburg's plantation.

The next day, we continued down the Georgia coast, coming near nighttime to the mouth of the Frederica River. I remembered the anchorages in the Frederica and decided to spend the night there. The sun was setting. We were running out of time.

In darkness, we made our way to where the river intersected with Dunbar Creek. We dropped anchor.

I cooked supper on the little alcohol stove, and we were safe for the night. I was traveling on my restored sailboat. I was alive. Mary was alive. But we were consumed with our fears. We were grasping for hope. And hope was like the Milky Way we lost in the fog two nights before. We may have known it was there. We may have seen it ourselves, just a short while earlier. But it was gone now.

At that time I did not know the story of Ebo Landing. Now that I know it, I may know the source of the spirits that haunted us that night. Because we truly were tormented and terrified in that lovely and tranquil place. The marsh grass swayed in moonlight. Tree frogs sang in the black, live-oak forest on shore. Dolphins blew in the darkness beside us.

But we were haunted by the ghosts of suicide. By the triumph of despair.

The story of the slaves who killed themselves in that place is so easy to believe. The story of the slaves who tried to walk to freedom across the water, while more poetic, is harder to believe. The story of the slaves who turned into birds and flew away, quacking in their magic language and leaving their hoes sticking up in the field, is beyond belief, is it not?

But which story of the Africans of Ebo Landing is true?

The Liberators

Letter from General T.W. Sherman, original commanding officer of Federal occupation forces in Port Royal, South Carolina, in the opening year of the American Civil War:

HEADQUARTERS EXPEDITIONARY CORPS,
Port Royal, S. C., December 15, 1861.

General LORENZO THOMAS,
Adjutant-General U. S. Army, Washington, D. C.:

SIR: For the information of the proper authorities, and for fear lest the Government may be disappointed in the amount of labor to be gathered here from the contrabands, I have the honor to report that from the hordes of negroes left on the plantations but about 320 have thus far come in and offered their services. Of these the quartermaster has but about 60 able-bodied male hands, the rest being decrepit, and women and children. Several of the 320 have run off. Every inducement has been held out to them to come in and labor for wages, and money distributed among those who have labored. The reasons for this apparent failure thus far appear to be these:

1st. They are naturally slothful and indolent, and have always been accustomed to the lash; an aid we do not make use of.

2d. They appear to be so overjoyed with the change of their condition that their minds are unsettled to any plan.

3d. Their present ease and comfort on the plantations, as long as their provisions will last, will induce most of them to remain there until compelled to seek our lines for subsistence.

T. W. SHERMAN,
Brigadier-General, Commanding.

P. S.-Besides those who have come in there are many still on the plantations employed in gathering cotton.

Order issued six months later by General Sherman's replacement, General David Hunter. This order was published in Beaufort three days before Robert Smalls commandeered the largest Confederate warship in Charleston harbor, and four days before General Hunter himself met Robert Smalls:

Head-quarters, Department of the South, Hilton Head, S.C. May 9, 1862

The three States of Georgia, Florida, and South Carolina, comprising the Military Department of the South, having deliberately declared themselves no longer under the protection of the United States of America, and having taken up arms against the said United States, it becomes a military necessity to declare them under martial law. This was accordingly done on the 25th day of April, 1862. Slavery and martial law in a free country are altogether incompatible. The persons in these three States---Georgia, South Carolina, and Florida---heretofore held as slaves, are therefore declared forever free.

David Hunter
Major-General Commanding
Ed. W. Smith Assistant Adjutant-General

The Sentry

There are dark secrets a man carries. I suppose we all got to carry secrets to keep going, just to go on living. But they eat at you. They come up in the night when you're trying to drift off. They come to you in the broad day when something somebody says, some situation that pops up, shines a light into that secret nobody else knows is there. Then you can't hardly think of nothing else but the secret, that shame, and you drift away from the conversation or the business you was in, and you can't get your head back around to it.

It wasn't even the conversation, really. It was just the look on that man's face, when Sully handed him the bill for the work we done, after six months of him a-adding this and that to the plans, and having us tear this out and redo that, and having us see the way his wife was a-henpecking him, and him not being man enough to stand up to it.

And then Sully handed him that bill, and he puffed his fat neck up like a rich man'll do when he's been caught out. And I knowed right then we wouldn't get paid. He got all red in the face and started getting the "I'm so damn much better than you trash" look in his eyes. I could almost guess what he was going to say next, but by that time, he had, without knowing it, shined a light right down into that shame and secret in my heart, and I wasn't even there in Walhalla no more. I was down in Charleston, on that waterfront, the morning after that thief stole the steamship thirty years ago.

I remember them officers when they walked out on that wharf in the early dawn light, and they looked at that empty opening on the wharf. The short, skinny one, the one that was the captain, seen the ship was gone. He looked like he'd been kicked in the head by a mule. He started turning red in the face and puffing up, and he started looking around for the one he was going to shift the blame to, and there I was.

I warn't nothing much more than a boy, walking that wharf in my uniform, which was still sharp and spiffy in them days of the war, with my rifle over my shoulder. I was too young and too green, I guess, to put the pieces together and calculate what had happened. I done seen the ship making steam. I done walked past it four times on my rounds in the early morning, as they was stoking the boiler and making steam. I could see the glow rising from her stacks. The coal smoke stank and burned my eyes as the breeze blowed it down along the wharf. I could see the niggers scuttling around on deck.

And I swear. I swear, I seen that captain standing in the wheelhouse twicet, leaning out the window, signaling them deckhands. He was wearing his uniform coat and a broad straw hat. I looked right at him and didn't see the truth. The truth that everyone knew by the end of that day, and don't a decent man in South Carolina want to admit to.

It was that nigger boat thief acting like the captain.

I seen it all happen. I walked past that ship four times before they got ready to cast off. My rounds was to walk all the way down to the point of the Battery and look out at the harbor and walk back down to Vanderhorst's wharf and then walk back. Down at Vanderhorst's wharf was the guardhouse. That dumbass boy lieutenant was sitting inside playing poker with four other officers, and every now and then, I guess when he won a hand and wanted to puff himself up a bit, he'd come outside when I got down there and take my report. I don't remember. I really don't remember, truth be told, if I ever told him about that ship making steam.

Then the deckhands cast the lines off the bollocks and was pulling them back on board. They got underway, and the captain (or the one I thought was the captain) gave the whistle signal. I was not a hundred yards away and seen all this in the darkness. I was coming back from the point of the battery. I seen the guardhouse door open in the distance, and that lieutenant step out and look down the wharf. And I seen him look for a while out into the darkness.

I heard the ship's wheels churning the water, and the steam blowing out from the pistons.   Kaaachoof! Then a splashing. Kaaachooof!

They say the nigger learned all the secret codes, is how he got out. I don't know. They didn't never tell me no codes. But the lieutenant, I seen him looking down the street and along those wharfs, and he warn't no more interested in what was going on than he had been in my reports all night, so I done always assumed the stories was right, and the whistle signal the thief give was the right one.

And I done took my lead from that lieutenant, when he ducked back into the guardhouse to get back to his poker game, with no more interest than if he had checked the weather outside. So, since I walked on down to where the *Planter* used to be tied up by that time, I stood with my rifle on my shoulder, in my spanking grey corporal's uniform, and watched as Robert Smalls and a band of runaways steamed away from the wharf in a stolen Confederate ship. That steamer was long and big as any six or seven houses. I watched it back slowly out from the wharf, and turn into the wind once it got clear out into the open water, and turn and head back up the Cooper River, which, as we learned later, was where they went to pick up their wenches and the little pickaninnies that went with them.

It's a shame a man can't hardly live with. To be a traitor almost. Or a coward. To know what a fool and a failure he was, when the chips was down, and his country was depending on him.

Of course, that was what that captain, the real captain of the *Planter*, was feeling when he was standing on that wharf in the early morning light, and his ship was gone. And that's when he turned and caught sight of me, and the memory of his look, that panicked look from the man who would be a laughingstock for the rest of his life, that look of a fool and coward looking at another fool and coward, dug up the secret one more time that morning in Walhalla thirty years later.

I couldn't even hear the cussing that man gave Sully that morning. I just watched Sully take it, red-faced and near murderous, the way I took that disgraced captain's cussing that morning thirty years ago on the wharf in Charleston.

The Conspirator

Well, and now they say Robert Smalls a tief, and they got the Honable Congressman on trial for it. The Charleston paper say he never even stole the *Planter*, that he hid in the hole while another man steer the boat. Which of course I know ain't so. I stood beside Robert in the wheelhouse while we passed Fort Sumter. I watched him blow the code on the whistle. He stuck the captain's straw hat out the pilot house door and waved to the sentries on Fort Sumter in the moonlight

Were Robert really calm as he looked, while I was standing behind him in the dark sweating? It were a cool, spring night, and I were running sweat like cutting rice in the noonday sun.

Robert stood outside that wheelhouse door where they coulda shot him down with a rifle. A jet black man with curly hair, standing in Captain Relyea's uniform wearing that big straw hat. It were still darkish, but you think one of them would notice it were a black man. You think somebody woulda figure out we done stole that boat and sent some sort of signal. It done been a hour since we left the wharf, and we took all that time to steam by a merchant ship half a mile down the waterfront to pick up the women and chilren.

I were shaking like a boy in a rice field when the overseer raise the whip. A little boy, not hardly big enough to do a day's work in a field. I remember the hot piss running down my legs into the stinking, gray mud of the rice field, and the way I shook, and the way I froze there when he swung that whip.

Across the dark water, I heard the voice: "Pass the *Planter!*"

And then, close after, maybe when I had stopped shaking, another voice, one of those upcountry twangs: "Blow them Yankees to hell!"

I thought he meant to kill us.

But Robert just give a wave, and shout, "Aye, Aye!" He step back into the wheelhouse, took the wheel, and steered us on.

The Spectator at Trial

The idiots of war. Oh God, I revile them. Patriotism is a cheap, easy emotion. It is the noble name they give their ignorance, prejudice, their basic human drive to pretend they could be murderers (though so very, very few actually act on that drive, given the weapon, the moral permission, the benediction of their countrymen, and even cash payment to do so).

Yet even one of these idiots, when he smells the first blood and shit and piss of his shredded fellows in a real battle, begins to change. He becomes something more like a real soldier. He becomes something like that butcher Grant. In his memoirs (yes, I've read them, keeping them locked in my desk drawer so no neighbor or visitor could see them) Grant called the scythe-like slaughter of war "execution." "We did much execution," he says, again and again, to describe the horror he had smelled and heard and waded through so many, many times. The horror that had been his doing. His command. His will. His pride. His strength. His cowardice. His greed. His sin. His horrible, unforgivable sin. So much more than sin. The screaming and mewling of the slaughtered idiots, so shortly before proud in their patriotic imbecility.

Not that the slaughter teaches them anything. They never stop. They never confess. They never prostrate themselves on the floor of the study (well, almost never), their lips moving across the dust of the wooden floor, as they beg the Almighty for forgiveness, for absolution, for some sign of redemption, from some respite from the screaming night terrors, from some break from the faces, the slaughtered, dismembered, shit-splattered idiots they led to their deaths. Rather than face that horrible moment with the Savior, and the even more horrible silence with which He responds, they carry on with the idiocy.

So I remember the idiot's scream from the ramparts of Sumter after I had given the *Planter* her pass: "BLOW THEM YANKEES TO HELL!"

Oh God, I cringed. To know this fool's future. To think of the ultimate futility.

And now I see the idiocy again, the unbroken pride, the futile patriotism of these men in Small's trial, some thirteen years later. He doesn't know I was the man who let him pass that night, the man who saw him in his captain's uniform and straw hat, with the poise and bearing of a fellow officer steering his own batch of idiots toward the slaughter.

I actually felt for him as I gave him permission to pass. I felt for the poor crew, who would surely be blown to pieces or captured sailing forth in the darkness to meet the blockade ships. I wondered if that captain, that fellow Confederate officer, had ever witnessed the horror before, or if he was one of the puffing idiots like that redneck who shouted from the ramparts.

Seeing Smalls here in court, swollen fatter by the years of politics and plunder, I can see how he pulled off his masquerade that night. There is nothing of the slave in him. He is as bold an idiot as the idiots who are framing him in this show trial. The officers of the Confederate army- holding on to their patriotism and their pride, even in defeat. They dress now in business suits. Smalls looks just like them, except for his black skin and his nappy hair. His suit is a bit finer than theirs, and it does make you wonder. How did a slave become so wealthy so fast? I've heard he lives in his master's former home.

But how do any of them live the way they do? They live off the plunder from the other idiots, I suppose. A whole nation of idiots who, having waded now through the guts of their countrymen, choose pride and power and murder rather than prostrating themselves for forgiveness. For deliverance. For freedom from the idiocy. For salvation. For escape.

After Small had passed in the *Planter*, when, against the thin line of dawn at the harbor's mouth, I saw the *Planter* strike the flag of the Confederacy and raise a large white bed sheet in its place, my idiot's eyes, for there was still some of the idiocy left in me, immediately thought this was some ruse to gain advantage on the blockading ships, perhaps to close the distance before the *Planter* opened fire in their suicide mission.

And then I realized what had happened. My mind thought just a bit beyond the obvious, and the obvious began to dawn on me. I gave the command to fire. My battery officers themselves, confused by the situation, took so long to comprehend. They couldn't wrap their understanding around the complexity of the situation, and then it took the enlisted men at their command an even longer while to find some understanding and to act. And no doubt, the idiot who had enjoined Smalls to "blow them Yankees to hell" was among this bewildered cohort at the guns.

By the time our guns fired, the *Planter* was out of range. The shells made geysers in her wake, spraying white against the dawn. Smalls, as sharp a wheelman as they say he was, took the unmarked, middle channel across the bar, the shortest way out of range of our guns from Moultrie or Wagner. How he took that steamer out through the mines, nets and shoals in the dark I can't tell you. I'd studied the secret charts of that harbor for hours. I know I couldn't have piloted a ship out in the conditions he ran. He was a clever man, and a bold one.

But now they've got him here in their courtroom, in his fine clothes, with his fat, rich-man's belly, and his ardent and learned attorney, and I wonder if he'll get away so clean this time.

The Fugitive

Ndemawnin light, we pull up side at wawship, wif em stars and stripe fline de light breeze, I bin sick.

Maybe demotion de sea. Rollin like a drunk man clambrin in bed with somepin on he mine. But I don't think so. I think I were fed we done drop into tuther world like uh fall out the sky on tuth.

It done only been couple hours since we leff uh dock. It done been free hour, maybe, since I rouse up Joshua outn he litter and come down Tradd Street, dragon he by the hand, and shushin he. I wuh sket. Sket to death. Sket UH death, but mo skettuh what they goin do to me and my chap ifn they ketch us. I done watch em whip and beat and bury live and hang and half-hang plenty runaway before. I knowed they crazy with war, now. They been crazy fed theyself, with the Yankee ship blockadin the hahbuh and the

Yankee army downaway. And they done got harder on the colored folk. They harder on the free colored, even, make em wear they pass around they neck outn public.

I never been on a ship. I holdin Joshua tight twix my knees and brace myself back again a wooden wall. The ship rumble and jolt and sprung and shook like it goin shake itself slam apart. I done pray to Jesus. I moanin and prayin to Jesus uh deliver me laud God awe mighty please.

Robert and John and tother men knowed what they wuh doin, I reckon. It wuh they work, evvy day, runnin that ship. I could see they fed, though. John and them other plenty fed. But I ain't see no fear in Robert. He young, and short, and slander, and a fine lookin black man. And he aint uh fed of nothin.

We done all greed we goin kill ourselve foe we let em take us.

It wuh only couple hour. But oh, what a tehble couple hour it wuh. It wuh dark, and later the thin line demawnin peer out over the ocean. Foe time the steam whistle blowed. Neach time I jump like it the trumpet uh judgment, and hug Joshua tightuh, and tremblin with fear. And I moanin pray to Jesus. Each time a whistle diffunt. Robert knowed the secret code each fort we passin by. He blow foe. He blow tree. He blow two. Whatever. He blow shotten long.

And uh daylight ginna fill the sky, we come up on the Yankee ship, rollin on it anchor chain. It mast rollin like uh crosses of Calvary gainst uh dawn, foe the sun brek over dorizon. I seen the soldier in they blue uniform leanin over the rail, strainin to see us.

And Hannah gannuh sang. She sung "Mazin Grace", and I, shakin with fear as I wuh, feel them tear ginnuh roll down my cheek, and I startuh sang, too. And then them others startuh sang, and we sung all the verse uh "Mazin Grace", and then we sung "Swing Low, Sweet Chariot", and then all the brethren sister startuh dance, dancin on the deck and cryin and sangin and shoutin like when the Spirit tek hole at a vival, and I bin fill with the Holy Ghost and praise the Laud and sung and dance and swung my Joshua and John round by the arm.

And them men in they blue uniform stare down to us holdin they rifle, like they uh watchin a minstrel show.

And Robert shout to the men in the blue uniform he thought Uncle Abe could use that ship. And they had the strangess look on they faces. I wonder they ever done seen colored folk a foe, comin fum wherever they come fum.

I wuh dancin and sangin and praisin the Laud, but oncet they come aboard, and point they rifle at us, I wuh took up with the fear again, and gan to feel sick again. And it wuhn't long a foe I frowed up. I frowed up right in front of em, it splatter on the deck at my feet, and them soldier in they blue uniform standing there with they rifle.

They tek us on board they ship, and they hold us on deck the longest time, round us with they uniform and they rifle, and they puzzle faces, while they tek Robert way to tuther part uh the ship. And I sho ain't feel free. I ain't feel no diffunt than I done feel befoe, scepter I wuh sket, and sick, and shakin, and that ship wuh rollin.

And them soldier look at us like we some kina strange animal, just unload off Noah ark. They ain't really look at us no diffunten any white person in Charleston ud look at you.

And I ain't feel free yet. I ain't feel free. But I wuh alive, and I ain't really spectuh be, and the world wuh altogether diffunt. It wuh altogether diffunt arrest of my life.

The Watch Commander

The morning Robert Smalls sailed the *Planter* out of Charleston harbor is perhaps my clearest memory of the war. Or maybe it is the one I most want to remember. That morning when the *Planter* steamed peacefully alongside us, with that group of darkies singing and dancing on its deck, and Robert Smalls in his Confederate captain's uniform as smiling and cock-proud as any cavalier, is the way I want the universe to be.

He was famous within forty-eight hours, I'm told. And I can see why. In the military, you see men's character laid bare regularly. The stress, terror and frustration of military life strip men of their ability to disguise themselves. In few weeks you know the real character of all those around you. But Smalls's character beamed across the muddy Atlantic waters when the *Planter* lay half a cable-length away.

His smile was contagious. It rose above all that was going on. We were trapped in a world of despair at that moment- week after week rolling at anchor in the murky, cold water off Charleston. The low, scrubby shoreline was all we had for scenery, punctuated by the forts and their batteries, just out of range. Week after week of boredom within half a mile of certain destruction. The awful gales of the winter and spring. Lying at anchor in an open roadstead with no protection. The stinging rain and spray. And the only respite a few days in the mosquito-filled fens and jungles of Port Royal or Hilton Head, with their voodoo-worshiping, jet-black contrabands speaking their unintelligible gibberish.

It was the darkest period of my life, but afterward, after Smalls came and opened up the assault on Charleston, the slaughter and the shelling and battle made life even worse. On the other hand, at least then there was the stimulation of the danger and fear. Before Smalls steamed out of that harbor, there was nothing but the tedium of despair.

I couldn't find any reason for the conflict. If these people wanted to be free, why shouldn't they be? Wasn't that the founding philosophy of our country? Self-determination? I had never seen any reason for our occupation and slaughter of these Confederates, who had only recently been my free countrymen enjoying their God-given rights to self-determination.

Seeing Smalls beaming his smile across the steel gray waters, though, in the most unlikely of conditions and most unlikely of circumstances, I could see then the darkies' dreams. I saw those strange people dancing and singing on the deck, and the grace and strength of their deliverer, and for a moment, I perceived some worth in the endeavor.

The Aide De Camp

There is a tree here, the live oak, that twists its limbs like a decoration in a faerie land, spreading farther and lower in all directions than the human imagination would lay it out, with graybeards of Spanish moss draping toward the ground. Underneath, a mottled shade disappears into a deep distance, cooling a green carpet of scrub palmetto, spiked and lush. Tiny island deer, black bears, and dreaded serpents move silently through this scrub. In the night, tree frogs ring with a voodoo cadence that transports the imagination to Africa and beyond.

Our camp lay amidst these live oaks, on a bluff overlooking a stretch of the green marsh grass and the tidal creek beyond. It was the most beautiful of locations, a welcome respite from a New Hampshire schoolmaster's existence. The winter had been mild- at times hot. No snow had come. And now the spring was brilliant with semi-tropical blossoms. The Negro women began to offer us shrimp and crabs along with the flounder and chickens they had been bringing us. I had begun to converse with them in their strange language, utterly incomprehensible to me at first, now becoming clearer as I recognized the underlying Englishness of its structure and vocabulary. They were a remarkably happy lot, having been abandoned some months earlier by their masters. They lived in the most rudimentary of natural conditions, in habitations barely differentiated from the ringing, live-oak forest and the long cotton fields filled with mist in the morning, beginning just now to shimmer with heat in the afternoon sun. There was nothing settled about our camp. It was a strange, temporary thing in a strange land.

The arrival of the *Planter* was just as alien, just as serendipitous. The steamer was of significant heft. It carried, in addition to its own armament, a collection of heavy artillery that had only recently been removed by the Confederates from one of their fortifications. The *Planter* was a river and coastal steamer, not really fit for long sea passages, but able to maneuver handily in the shallow, opaque waters of that region.

The *Planter*'s story spread rapidly through the camp. The news took fire among the blacks, as if it were the most unbelievable of revelations. One might imagine the spread of the Resurrection story among Jesus' followers. There was a look of utter incredulity, mixed at once with the most fervent desire to believe and the hope that the horrible reality had, if only this once, contrary to all understanding and experience, been breached.

I watched the crew of the *Planter* shuffle off under guard, moving as any of the myriad, small groups of contrabands who wandered into our camp each day. But in the rear of the procession strode Smalls. A very young man of diminutive stature and slight build, he didn't really stride. He rolled off the gangplank like a man who was stepping in to his rightful existence, the one for which he had been destined since his creation.

In a hastily swollen army, built of necessity from a population of farmers and attorneys, shopkeepers and schoolmasters, one sees much artificial swagger. The uniform, the unearned rank, the unaccustomed command lead to comic displays of puffery and preening. But there was nothing of this in Smalls.

General Hunter summoned me to attend the debriefing in his headquarters, a sprawling plantation house in the shade of the live oaks. I was in the General's office when Smalls was introduced. Smalls had a seducing glint in his eyes. He had an aura of incipient success about him. I found myself instantly liking him.

As he was presented, he strode right up to the edge of the General's desk and stuck his black hand enthusiastically across the desk to be shaken. The General, whom I had never seen shake hands before, looked down at the proffered hand with a momentary look of amazement which he was unable to disguise. He quickly regained his composure, firmly grasped Small's hand, and shook it with enthusiasm and a grin.

Smalls discussed his escape and his crew, which included his wife and children. It was so pleasing to be around a young man of such charisma and intelligence. One found oneself pulling for the chap at every turn of the conversation, silently cheering as he answered each question with the humility and quick-wittedness to further win his audience.

Smalls did not speak to us as the other Negroes spoke, although over the months to come, I observed that he was completely bilingual and could speak to his fellow coloreds in their pidgin as if it were his mother tongue. He told his story to the General as would any white man from that region in possession of education and good breeding. I later was astonished to learn Smalls could neither read nor write. He appeared to have had some special background, some rare upbringing that separated him from the mass of the slaves we encountered.

I have often read and heard that Smalls was a mulatto, fathered and raised by his owner. That might, perhaps, explain some of this self-possession and demeanor as he was debriefed by a United States general. Yet I must admit that I never saw any white features in the man. He was as darkly complected as any of the other slaves I encountered on Hilton Head or a Port Royal. His hair was as kinky as any full-blooded Negro of those sea islands. And his features were as African as theirs. If one spends much time at all with these people, one quickly learns just how remarkably distinct their features are from those of European descent. I once encountered a contraband who was an albino Negress. The unfortunate young woman was quite odd-looking. With skin as white as mine, and far blonder hair, she nevertheless had the flattened nose, prominent brow, and other facial features of the African. As often as we encountered true mulattoes in South Carolina, I find it difficult to believe that Smalls himself had any European blood in his veins.

General Hunter's interest suddenly rose as Smalls discussed the provenance of the artillery pieces the *Planter* carried as deck cargo. The day previous to Smalls's escape, the *Planter* loaded the pieces from one of the forts guarding the entrance to the Stono River, just south of Charleston. The rebels had decided to abandon their positions guarding that unnavigable inlet.

Smalls, however, said he knew the inlet quite well and had passed through it often in the years before the war.

The General asked Smalls if he felt he could navigate the inlet today, and Smalls displayed no hesitation in saying he could.

Thus was the idea of an assault upon the Stono quickly hatched, and a new front opened in the seat of war in South Carolina.

The Seller

I always liked that boy, from the time I first met him. Although Hannah and her mother had been dear to me as servants in our household, there was the inevitable distance one feels between slave and master. There was the divide that had to be maintained. But this young man tempted me to step a bit closer to the divide. He was open, quick-witted, and an able worker. Those who employed him along the waterfront and as a wheelman had the highest confidence in him.

His dogged interest in Hannah mystified me. She was noticeably older than he, and she already had two children- quite obviously fathered by some other slave. But he was devoted to her, and I was pleasantly surprised when he asked if he could marry her. I consented, after consulting with his owner, Mr. McGee of Beaufort.

McGee seemed to think highly of Robert, too. He had sent the boy to Charleston some seven or eight years earlier to work for hire. McGee undoubtedly felt the young man would be a good earner for him. His return correspondence to me seemed to betray genuine concern for the boy's welfare and happiness.

Robert married Hannah and moved into a shack behind our house, where she could continue her domestic duties. He was often away from home aboard whatever steamer he was working on. I would see him walking into our garden at the most random hours, when his ship returned to port and released him from his duties on board. I rarely heard squabbling or fighting from that shack.

Nothing could have prepared me for Robert's next proposal. I suppose it was the white blood in him. There's nothing more disgusting to me than a man who would lie with his slave, but that's neither here nor there. It happens enough, and what comes of it is something like poor Robert, a part-white soul living in a slave's body.

Robert proposed buying Hannah and her brood from me. Although I didn't allow him to see it, his proposal pained me to the core. He was such a decent and upright man, I thought. I had always cared so much for Hannah. I wanted her to be happy with this man. No one could possibly dislike young Robert. I have never known a man, black or white, with the charismatic attraction of that young fellow.

There was ample precedent of free coloreds owning slaves, even buying their women and children. But I doubted there was any standing in law for a slave to buy another slave. Nevertheless, I wanted to help Robert and to do whatever I could to support and sustain Hannah's marriage to him. Robert largely lived as a free colored anyway. Such was his relationship with his owner, this McGee, who well may have been his very father, that Robert lived his life almost as his own man. And it was not entirely outside my imagination that the institution of slavery might not outlive us. Certainly I recognized the possibility that it might not outlive Robert and Hannah.

So I made an agreement to sell him his wife and her children. I drew up a bill of sale for seven hundred dollars and took a down payment from him of one hundred dollars. Where and how he had amassed that down payment I have no idea. It never occurred to me he might be a thief. There was nothing about the man that ever gave me the slightest suspicion such behavior was in his character. It goes, of course, to show how wrong we may be when we pretend we can see into other men's souls.

I drew up the papers and took his money, realizing I myself might be breaking the law in having drawn up such a contract. But who would know? I intended to honor the spirit of the contract as long as the two of them lived under my protection. The transaction seemed to give Hannah and Robert the greatest joy and pride. There was no possibility he would ever try to get legal title to the three of them for the purpose of a sale. And there was the distinct possibility that this earnest, industrious, and thrifty young man would deliver me further payments over the years to come. My emotional attachment to Hannah, and, by extension, to her children, was such that I doubt I would ever have been able to sell them to another man for any consideration. I was not sacrificing property that was ever likely to bring me or my descendants financial gain.

Oh, vanity! Such calculation. Such careful business planning. Where did it get me? Ruined by war. Destitute. Unable to support my own family. This Robert, having stolen from me my property, now rides through Beaufort, I read in the Charleston papers, in the finest of carriages, in his fancy clothes, as if he were a king. I hear he owns McGee's home now. Poor McGee is dead.

I have read that Robert had on his person the balance of the seven-hundred-dollar payment when he stole the *Planter*. I doubt now that he ever intended to pay me that money. Thievery is, after all, so much more convenient than honor. And in time of calamity and war, thieves are transcendent.

I met Robert on more than one occasion immediately after the war. At the war's end, he had piloted the *Planter* back into Charleston, overloaded to the gunwales with drunken coloreds and carpetbag-toting Yankees. He strutted through town as the black-faced conqueror.

Oh, he was most gracious, most kind to me. He has lost nothing of the charisma. Even in defeat, I could not help but like the man. I could not help but celebrate his freedom and happiness in my heart. And Hannah seemed as almost as happy as he. Nothing in me begrudged her this.

The money I was owed turned out to be utterly uncollectable.

They seemed to be such decent people. They were people I loved. I look into my own soul, I admit I love them still. You've got to be a damn fool to love a nigger.

The Commander

I was commanding the third steamer to enter the Stono. Smalls, the escaped slave, was piloting his stolen vessel, the *Planter*, in the lead of the assault. I kept two sounding men casting lead on either side of the bow. The sea was a glassy calm, with a three-to-four-foot swell from the northeast peaking ominously in the shallows and the tidal currents of that treacherous inlet. We entered on a rising tide, hoping it would carry us off if we grounded.

Smalls moved his steamer with skill and confidence, and we followed in tight formation behind him. I was sweating in the steamy, early-summer heat, which seemed unbearable then, although it was nothing compared to what would come in the months ahead.

From our initial positions offshore, Smalls led us some two miles to the south of the inlet, and then close in along the beach. The dark, sea-island forest lay unbroken along the dunes. I expected fire from the rebels at any point along that run. But they had apparently abandoned this shoreline, and we passed unmolested.

When the sounding men called two fathoms, my muscles tensed. I had two steamers ahead of me, but we had the deepest draft of that small fleet by at least three feet. When the sounding men began calling one and a half, I waited for the thud of the keel on the bar. But it never came.

We passed the bar, turned to port into the inlet, and within minutes we were in South Carolina.

Here I expected a fierce battle, and I feared what would happen if the *Planter* were disabled and Smalls rendered incapable of leading us back out of that inlet. The river inside was wide enough for maneuvering, but not wide enough to evade artillery fire.

Broad expanses of salt marsh stretched upstream before us. There were sea islands close by on either side of the inlet, covered at these extremes with sand dunes, sea oats, and scrub. A wide river branched off to the north. Another river branched to the south a mile or so in.

Smalls led us on on a middle course up the Stono. We could see fortifications on a small island in the salt marsh to our north. As Smalls had reported, they were abandoned. Soon the riverbank to port was covered in the deep forest again. Still we encountered no enemy fire. Within an hour, we had steamed some five or six miles inland, and I began to wonder if we might land our troops at the very verges of Charleston. But as we approached a forested shore on the starboard side, the first artillery shells began to thunder into the river ahead of us. Smalls stopped the *Planter*, and we backed a half a mile or so down the river.

After some consultation, we anchored in the Stono a mile beyond the range of those Confederate guns on James Island. We had behind us an expanse of river sufficient to hold our entire fleet, miles of unoccupied land on the south and west side of the river, and the sea island on the north side of the river entrance. We were within seven miles of the city of Charleston. And we had not suffered a single casualty.

Smalls had advanced Federal forces farther in a morning than we had advanced in months of campaigning.

The Great Emancipator

President Lincoln's Response to General Hunter's proclamation freeing slaves in South Carolina, Georgia, and Florida. Lincoln issued this response ten days after General Hunter issued his proclamation, and six days after Robert Smalls escaped from Charleston harbor with the Planter:

By the President of The United States of America.

A Proclamation.

Whereas there appears in the public prints, what purports to be a proclamation, of Major General Hunter, in the words and figures following, to wit:

(Lincoln inserted General David Hunter's proclamation freeing the slaves here.)

And whereas the same is producing some excitement, and misunderstanding: therefore

I, Abraham Lincoln, president of the United States, proclaim and declare, that the government of the United States, had no knowledge, information, or belief, of an intention on the part of General Hunter to issue such a proclamation; nor has it yet, any authentic information that the document is genuine. And further, that neither General Hunter, nor any other commander, or person, has been authorized by the Government of the United States, to make proclamations declaring the slaves of any State free; and that the supposed proclamation, now in question, whether genuine or false, is altogether void, so far as respects such declaration.

I further make known that whether it be competent for me, as Commander-in-Chief of the Army and Navy, to declare the Slaves of any state or states, free, and whether at any time, in any case, it shall have become a necessity indispensable to the maintenance of government, to exercise such supposed power, are questions which, under my responsibility, I reserve to myself, and which I can not feel justified in leaving to the decision of commanders in the field. These are totally different questions from those of police regulations in armies and camps.

On the sixth day of March last, by a special message, I recommended to Congress the adoption of a joint resolution to be substantially as follows:

Resolved, That the United States ought to co-operate with any State which may adopt a gradual abolishment of slavery, giving to such State Pecuniary aid, to be used by such State in it discretion to compensate for the inconveniences, public and private, produced by such change of system.

The resolution, in the language above quoted, was adopted by large majorities in both branches of Congress, and now stands an authentic, definite, and solemn proposal of the nation to the States and people most immediately interested in the subject manner. To the people of those states I now earnestly appeal. I do not argue. I beseech you to make the arguments for yourselves. You can not if you would, be blind to the signs of the times. I beg of you a calm and enlarged consideration of them, ranging, if it may be, far above personal and partisan politics. This proposal makes common cause for a common object, casting no reproaches upon any. It acts not the Pharisee. The change it contemplates would come gently as the dews of heaven, not rending or wrecking anything. Will you not embrace it? So much good has not been done, by one effort, in all past time, as, in the providence of God, it is now your high privilege to do. May the vast future not have to lament that you have neglected it.

In witness whereof, I have hereunto set my hand, and caused the seal of the United States to be affixed.

Done at the City of Washington this nineteenth day of May, in the year of our Lord one thousand eight hundred and sixty-two; and of the Independence of the United States the eighty-sixth.

Abraham Lincoln

In August, 1862, after Robert Smalls led U.S. Forces into the Stono River, General Hunter sent Smalls to

Washington to meet with President Lincoln. Immediately following this meeting, Secretary of War Stanton issued an order allowing enlistment of blacks in U.S. Army. Within a month, Lincoln issued a proclamation promising to free all slaves in the Confederacy as of the first the new year. On January 1, 1863, Lincoln issued the proclamation now known as the Emancipation Proclamation.

The Secretary

Spending substantial time each day in the presence of the President, I quite easily laid aside in my considerations the extraordinary strength of his own character and personality. He was a man, much like any other, going through his work in a most unusual occupation, but behaving much as any shopkeeper or livery owner or lawyer might behave during the course of an ordinary day. Often tired. At times inarticulate. Sometimes peevish and petty. Often visibly confused or frightened. Always struggling to disguise those emotions from others.

Yet it was never lost on me that he was a most extraordinary man, and he could, when he so chose, and when the Almighty blessed him with the necessary grace, simply amaze those with whom he was conversing, transmigrating the business at hand, and calling men to some place they would not go on their own.

This grace and force sometimes presented themselves in his interlocutors, also. For there in the President's office, matters of the greatest import were often under consideration, and I found myself thinking the men who sat or stood in that place, at times, rose far beyond their ordinary powers of thought, speech, and consideration, and spoke as if infused with a spirit that came from some place outside themselves.

The meeting of the President with Robert Smalls was one of those occasions. Smalls was at this time quite famous, and I enjoyed a substantial thrill of anticipation at actually getting to meet him. I could sense some of this thrill in the President.

I was surprised by how short the colored man was, especially next to Lincoln. I had been informed that Smalls was a complete illiterate, and I assumed the white man who accompanied him would do much of the talking. Smalls was quite young and had escaped from bondage only a few weeks before. I anticipated he would be as deferential and quiescent as the steward who brought us coffee when the President summoned with his pull cord. Smalls was a famous and dashing man, much interviewed, celebrated, and written about in the papers. And he had boldly stolen a Confederate steamer from the middle of their most heavily fortified port. But here he would find himself in as unaccustomed a situation as if he had suddenly been transported to the surface of the moon, I thought.

That was not what happened at all. Smalls's white companion, a Reverend French I believe, did not particularly interest the President. Instead, the president was full of questions about Smalls's recent exploits, about his seizing of the *Planter* and his leading our fleet into Stono Inlet. And Smalls told his story with a plainspoken straightforwardness, humility, and boldness that instantly captured the imagination of the President. Here was one extraordinary, ordinary man speaking to another, and there was an instant affinity, an instant chemistry.

Smalls's story was remarkable. It was as if the steward had, instead of bringing the coffee when the President pulled his chord, entered the room and challenged the President on the strategy for campaigning the Army of the Potomac. I was terrified as I listened to Smalls's tale, the certainty of torture and death if their escape failed, the unlikelihood of passing the forts in the night with their system of coded signals, the impossibility of navigating the mine field in the dark with the strong tidal currents sweeping them toward the bank.

Every man in the room listened, the President included, with the awe of one who knows the speaker is far more courageous than he.

Was Smalls simply too young to understand the impossible audacity of his deed? Or was he a man of more daring than any I had ever met?

How rarely had I seen the President overwhelmed by a visitor to his office? Usually, he listened patiently to the generals, the cabinet secretaries, the senators, the famous orators, and then, when he had tired of their posturing and puffing, he would slide one of his frontiersman homilies across the room to let them know just how little he was impressed.

But listening to this young slave, the President sat transfixed.

General Hunter had sent Smalls to advocate for his initiative to enlist freed coloreds in the army. The President was not in the least inclined to listen to this counsel, I feel. He had never felt colored men were the equals of white men, and he worried often, in my hearing, about what would become of these people when slavery was abolished. His concerns extended to the care, feeding, gainful employment, and governing of freed slaves. A week or so before Smalls's visit, the President had addressed a group of freed coloreds in his office, exhorting them to separate themselves from the white race and lead their brethren to a new colony in Central America. In no way, I feel, did he envision dressing these poor, ignorant men in uniforms and arming them for modern warfare.

Yet here was a man who had weeks before been an illiterate, oppressed bondsman, trapped in Charleston, South Carolina, as unnoticed and uncared for as any of his fellow servants, and he was before us transformed into the boldest warrior in the nation, a man who had shown more courage, initiative, and accomplishment than all the generals who had heretofore entered this office.

The President sat though most of his meetings politely and inquisitively, but with little prospect of his core beliefs changing. On those occasions when I had seen him reverse himself, the change came slowly and deliberately, for a truly open mind, as the President certainly had, can be changed with persuasive argument.

But never before had I seen President Lincoln astonished.

The Curious

I went to see a lecture by Robert Smalls, the dashing Negro hero, at the Union Club during the war. I had read a number of articles about his daring escape with his steamship from Charleston harbor, under the very guns of the Confederates. I was not really prepared for what I found.

Smalls was a compact and slender young man, nothing in appearance like the rotund Congressman I met in later years. He had a shiny, new suit of clothes, somewhat a challenge to come by in those war years, and he was well-groomed and well-mannered. But his appearance, as a jet-black man with shining, white eyes and teeth, and his parted hair rising from his head like a sage bush, was rather startling, frankly. It was as if a wild man from the jungle had been dressed meticulously by a Fifth Avenue haberdasher for an evening on the town.

When he stood to speak, there was no fear in him. There was no visible stage fright, even though the assemblage must have contained some four- to five-hundred persons. He spoke in a loud, clear voice, with an infectious smile and an immediately disarming sense of humor. He had then, at that young age, the politician's innate ability to make you feel instantly his friend, and to make you feel you agreed with him in all things.

He spoke with the accent and the clear diction of a Southern gentleman. One might close one's eyes and think Jefferson Davis were addressing the meeting. The sight was so incongruous!

Smalls seemed to harbor no animosity towards those who had held him in bondage. I found this interesting. I had attended lectures by abolitionists in the past, where the horrors of slavery, the depravity and cruelty of the lash, the indiscriminate rupturing of family ties, were recounted vividly by those who had survived them first hand.

Yet Smalls spoke not at all of these aspects of his earlier life. I wondered if he had in fact led some sort of charmed existence in his youth, one that allowed him to speak and think and act as if he were a free man rather than a slave.

His earlier career had been as a seaman, first as a rigger, then as a deck hand, and for many years as a pilot (or a wheelman, as he called it) on steamers along the coasts of South Carolina, Georgia, and Florida. In this manner, although he was a slave, he seems to have become accustomed to the authority of command and decision-making. He spoke with all the confidence of a sea captain, of one who has faced challenges far beyond those presented by the drawing room or the lecture hall.

He was basking in his newfound notoriety, and one could see an occasional absence of humility. As he was such a young man, it was easy to overlook. It would have been less appealing in an older man.

The other thing I remember from his lecture was his religiosity. The man seemed to have the most profound Christian faith. I understand the only religion allowed by the slave holders among their Negro charges is that based upon the Apostle Paul's admonition to slaves to serve their masters willingly. As Paul was a slave of Christ, so should the loyal Negro be to his white master.

Yet Smalls seemed to hold to a Christianity that did not need him as a slave. He described his fervent prayer as he piloted the steamship out of the harbor, past the forts and mines that would almost certainly blow him and his fellow fugitives to eternity. As he described the situation, it was the most desperate of endeavors. There was virtually no way they could escape. Any rational man could see that, and Smalls seemed to be the most rational of men. If, by some small chance, they were not killed by the guns or the exploding mines, they would have been publicly tortured to death upon their capture. Indeed, because of this, they took an oath not to be captured alive.

Yet Smalls's faith and his constant prayer overcame this rationality and this fear. There was in the man a most irrational belief in deliverance by the Almighty- the same Almighty who had delivered him, at his birth, into servitude, and who had held him, his loved ones, his forebears, in said condition quite without hope of recourse up to that point.

Now Smalls had taken matters into his own hands, and he prayed throughout his journey for deliverance by this same God.

Against all reason, Smalls attributed his deliverance entirely to that God. He attributed none of it to his own daring, courage, and skill.

Smalls said these things with the conviction of the revivalist giving his testimony. He meant to convert the incredulous in the audience, to bring any lingering unbelievers back to Christ.

I must admit, for the moment, at least in my case, he came close to succeeding.

For years afterward, I have envied him that faith. I find myself conversing with him in my imagination as the years go by, probing and arguing the great questions of existence with that young man who believed so strongly and so absolutely.

I wonder now, in his old age- if he is still alive- if he still holds to that faith- after his destruction at the hands of his enemies- after the near re-enslavement of his people- after nearly every prominent national politician has adopted the stance that he and his fellow Negroes are an inferior and dangerous race that must be kept in their proper place, deprived of most of the rights granted to them by an all-consuming war, constitutional amendments, and- can I resist the irony?- by their Almighty God himself.

The Ironclad Officer

The ironclad warship *Keokuk* was like a giant tomb. In the summer, when I first came aboard, it was hot as an oven. I imagined, the first time I went below and the ship made steam and the engine started turning her screw propeller, that this must be exactly what it is like to find yourself in hell. How did I go from a farm in Indiana to this rolling, stinking, clanging hell off the coast of South Carolina? To come out on deck for my short respite in fresh air was a deliverance like a reprieve from the inferno. The seasickness, from which I had suffered terribly since we left Philadelphia aboard the warship *Avenger*, had begun to subside in me. I no longer wretched at the rail as the crew laughed. Now I just felt a misery deep in my bones, and it was all I could do to focus some small bit of strength on my duties. I gasped desperately at the steaming, hot air. I looked across the oily, grey swells to the beach and dunes along the shore, toward the hideous pile of sand and logs, bristling with artillery, that was Fort Wagner.

We suffered in the heat throughout the fall, really. I despaired whether winter would ever come to this part of the world. But by December, it had come, and we gladly sheltered below in that stifling ironclad from the wind and spray of the first winter gales.

We had spent late summer, fall, and the beginning of winter on station off Charleston, forming the blockade. Except for our occasional, usually pointless pursuit of blockade runners in the dark, we lay at anchor, rolling in the seas, keeping on a head of steam, for day after endless day. We scraped. We chipped. We painted. Once a week we fired the guns. Firing those guns inside that tomb was like sticking your head in a cauldron and setting off a stick of dynamite in your teeth.

Our coaling and watering calls in Port Royal were a welcome relief. We occasionally got a day of liberty there, which allowed us nothing more than a stroll and a visit to a storefront or two in the little port of Beaufort. The town at that time was full of Negro camp followers. The local whites had fled. Soldiers and sailors had to be fed and supplied, and some of the sharpest Negroes looked to it.

That's where I first saw Mr. Smalls. He was working at his dry goods store when a fellow officer and I went in looking for tobacco. It was strange to see a colored man standing behind his own store counter. I'd never seen such before. But Mr. Smalls was a pleasant, straightforward man, it seemed to me then.

We knew an attack was coming by Thanksgiving. You could see the number of ironclads in the area growing. And you could see the earnestness in higher ranking officers. Mr. Smalls had come aboard before Thanksgiving as a pilot. He had formerly been a pilot for the Confederates. The word on the ship was that he knew the waters of Charleston Harbor better than any man.

We all took a liking to Mr. Smalls. He was a man of good humor. He had a kind word for everyone he met. He treated the officers almost as equals, but not in a way that would offend. He treated the sailors as equals, too, but not in the way that would encourage them to take him lightly. He was quick to laugh and quick with a joke himself, which he would share with an officer or sailor. After he told a joke, he would break out in the biggest belly laugh, his white teeth flashing.

The morning of the attack, the officers were in a fine state of tension. We were assembled on deck, and we knew we were steaming in to battle. We could see our fleet of ironclads rolling around us in the grey, December swells, black smoke rising from their stacks as they made steam.

I was the most scared I've ever been in my life. I can't even describe my fear.

I remember the pitching deck and the cold spray as the anchor chain clanked aboard. I remember the boatswain calling a cadence and the fear in his voice as he did.

We could see the other ironclads steaming into a line ahead of us. The rebels could see the attack forming up, too. There would be no surprise in this, no trying to sneak through like the blockade runners in the night. I remember those columns of black smoke arcing off in the breeze, terrible black smoke as the ironclads arranged themselves into a line and headed towards the bar.

If Mr. Smalls knew the harbor better than any man in the Navy, why did they have him in the last ship in line? I remember thinking that.

We were below, with the hatches bolted shut, and the gun ports opened, when I heard the first gunfire. It rolled across the water like thunder. Boom... Boom... Boom... Spaced apart at first, and then coming thicker and thicker, like a thunderstorm gathers and strengthens as it nears you. Through our gun port, I could see Fort Wagner, built of sand and logs. I could see the guns fire before I heard the boom. First a spout of flame, then a cloud of smoke, then the sound of the gun, then the splash of the ball just short of us.

The Waterboy

I wuh with Robert on the ineclad *Kekuk* when they tack Charleston hahber. They wuh a whole fleet of ineclads tack that hahber that day, in a straight line, one afta thudder. Them black ship, steamin out black smoke, it blowin in the winter wind. I never forget id. I thought it wuh goin be over that day, that we ud win the war and take over Charleston and all the brethren sistuh be free.

Robert wuh a pilot in the Navy, and he tuck me long on that battle. They had me carrin water, was all, so I seen all what happen.

Them gun from Moss Island staht firin fust. You see the flame leap out, and then the smoke, then you hear the gun, then bout tha time you see the ball hit the water. It thow up a cloud uh water and steam something awe full, bout fitty feet high. And quick as we in range, they staht firin boom boom boom one right atter dudder.

And them ship steamin on in a line, black, with that black smoke blowin.

And I don know why they put Robert in the last ship, when he the one that knowed the hahber bettern any them Yankee. They aint never been in there, when Robert the one done laid mos the mine and schung them net and knowed that whole hahber like the backa he hand.

They staht firin fum Sullivans, too, and then out fum Fote Sumptuh. And then that whole hahber lit up with fire and smoke, and the ball roaring this way and that, and it sound like the enduh the world. Them ball shriek through the air like a screamin haint in the fahst at night, when you know them haints is flyin and screamin and lookin for soul to steal.

And I watch them sailor get sket. I wuh plenty sket myseff. But them fahmboy from up North, they skettuh death. When I us a chap, I learnt how not to be so sket. You see them people whip and hang and beat and drag thew the screet and what all, and it do sompin to you atter while, and they caint hardly scare you like a normal man. I watch my daddy beat down to his knees when I a little chap, beat down in the mud by that ovuhseeuh, whip him till he bleedin all over, roun top his head.

I done see a alligator eat a boy out in uh rice field one mawnin, grab that boy and he let out one yep and then he underwater and you aint see nothin but black water trouble and trouble and trouble. A slave see enough thing you caint hardly scare him like them poor white boy us sket.

And once all the fote staht to firin, thing start to go bad for them ineclad. The fust un started gettin all tangle up in the net them rebel laid cross the hahber. Robert laid bunch a them net heseff. Dem ineclad got to turnin sideway and hung up and all bine up. And they staht firin they gun, too, but they too far out to hit them fote, and they just firin and turnin and all foul up.

And by this time the noise sompin awe full. And I seen some them sailor so scared they caint move, they just stand there with they eye wide open like they seen the haint pohin out uh hell. And that Captain, he mo than a little sket heseff, and Robert say let him take the ship in, he can get the ship in the hahber heseff, and the Captain he say go head.

And Robert, he aint sket uh nothin. I aint never seen him sket uh nuthin, and he tol that wheelman was steerin that ship get over heah on the lahbud, run round them ship on the lahbud, and he told that engine man give he flank speed, and we went boilin on past them ship, and we head right in towed Fote Sumptuh.

And them rebel start firin like somebody done stuh up a hornet nest. Like somebody done tow up four or five hornet nest at oncet. It wuh like, well, I caint describe it.

And them ball start to hittin that ine ship, and it wuh like you inside a bell and God awe mighty swing a giant sledge hard as he can, and that ship bouncin this way and thudder evy time one of them balls hit.

It like the end of the world.

And Robert, he commence to get mad.

Them other, they skettuh death. I seed men peein theyselves and the pee runnin down they legs, and they white as haints. And they this one boy done curl up in the corner on the deck, huggin his knee and cryin. And he jerk and scream out evy time one uh them ball hit.

And Robert he tell em start firin them gun. And he mad. He the maddest I evuh see a man. And he pull that ship right up front of Fote Sumptuh and he tell em fire the goddam gun, blow that goddam fote outta water. And they fire them gun fast as they could load em and light um, and the noise uh make you deaf. Like bein inside a thunderstorm with the lightning and the thunder coming out you nose. It wuh hell. I tell you, it wuh hell.

And them rebel, they gots to turn they gun down to shoot at the *Kekuk*. Robert take that ship right up to em, and we firin them gun jus fast as them sailor could load em. And them ball hittin that ship like ringin a lahm bell when they a fire in town, only each one, it like God awe mighty done hit you with the hammer of judgment, and it knock you clear cross that ship, them gun in the fote so close now. And Robert, he just madder and madder. He goan take Charleston hahber, and aint nobody goan stop him.

And they one ball hit that ship, and bust the wheelman head wide open standin next to Robert, and Robert splattuh with the blood and the brain that wheelman, and then Robert grab the wheel and he keep on goan. He like a crazy man. He aint havin none of it.

And we stay in that hahber, I don't know, it might a been five, six year. It might a been a hole lifetime. It might a been two tree lifetime. It might a been all the lifetime evuh been live. It like time done stop. It like I been in hell and seen the debbil, and all them demon, and all them haint, and I aint uh fed of nothing now I live thew that.

And them other ship aint come in like Robert done. They all stay out at the bar and aint come in close. And Robert up underneath that fote fightin like he the angel uh God fightin the debbil heself, but that fote ain't goan nowhere. It just bouncin them ball off. You see the brick a flyin when them ball hit, but it aint done nothin to them rebel.

And atter while, atter long, long while, a long time atter evvy man on that ineclad done give up hope and knowed he wuh a dead man, atter while even Robert knowed we wuh gettin blowed to bit. Them ball wuh hittin like they beatin us with the butt end a cannon. Finely Robert turn and steam back outta the hahber, and by that time all them other ineclad done turn and run out ahead of us.

We got back out in the ocean, with the rest the fleet, and that *Kekuk*, she wuh done blowed apot. She wuh takin on water, and we fought the rest that day trying to keep the water outtn her and keep her floatin, and Robert, he fought the hardess, and I saw what it mean to he, and I work like I doin the laud's work down in that ship to keep that ocean out.

But we cant keep the whole ocean outn that ship. That ineclad done been blowed to bit. I wuh up on the other ship when it finely went down. And Robert the last man on the *Kekuk*. He jump off that ship and swim away when she go down the water for good.

That Robert, I tell you. He wunt skettuh nothin. That man aint uh fed of nothin scepter laud God awe mighty in he glory.

Uncle Romulus

Jim Huger put us up for the night at the Carolina Yacht Club. Tom and Mac and I were down for a week on the boat, cruising the South Carolina coast. We'd asked Huger to come with us, but he couldn't schedule the time off. Instead, he invited us to tie up at his Yacht Club, so we could all have dinner together downtown in the Holy City. As any tourist knows, Charleston is called the Holy City (with some irony) because of all the church steeples in its historic district.

The Yacht Club is on East Bay Street in the historic district, right next to the Battery. I knew that was roughly where Smalls had been docked on the *Planter* the night he stole it. An historical marker on the East Battery wall, right beside the Yacht Club entrance, says the *Planter* was at a wharf about 150 yards east, which would put it almost exactly where we were moored in my 35-foot sailboat (a larger, slightly newer model than the one in which I had visited Ebo Landing a few years earlier. Times had gotten a little better for me.)

We sat in the cockpit drinking rum and tonic that evening. The sun settled on a lovely, May afternoon. From that position, you can see down the length of Charleston Harbor, past Castle Pinckney on the left and Fort Sumter on the right, straight out the channel into the ocean. In 1862, that would have been the middle of three channels running over the bar from Charleston Harbor. But the other two are mostly gone now. The north channel, sneaking out past Sullivan's island, is completely blocked off by the jetties guarding the harbor entrance. The south channel, which had been the main harbor channel in the first few centuries of Charleston's history, and the channel through which I imagine Smalls steaming in the *Keokuk's* assault on the harbor, still exists to some extent. There is a minuscule opening in the south jetty, marked by two buoys, which would let a smaller boat exit through this undredged channel. On the charts, you can see the underwater contours of a natural channel running outside the jetty, along the coast of Morris Island, to what was once the natural harbor bar.

The site of Fort Wagner on Morris Island is now under water, erosion having consumed it within a couple of decades of the Civil War. But Fort Sumter, of course, still stands as a National Monument, with its flags flying and its tour boats coming and going. Castle Pinckney has been purchased by the Sons of Confederate Veterans, who are reconstructing the fortifications there. They have installed a flagpole to fly a large Confederate flag over the island.

But that is neither here nor there.

Sitting at the Yacht Club transient dock, almost exactly at the spot where Smalls had sat with his co-conspirators and hatched the plan for his escape, you can look straight out the channel. I saw a huge auto transport ship (coming to pick up BMW's for export), making its way inbound on the old middle channel, and I realized from this position Smalls could have handily seen the Federal ships of the blockade fleet as he stood on board the *Planter*. He was the master of that vessel in reality, but at the same time a slave with no rights, no freedom, no father, no name. (Many historical sources speculate he was simply known on the waterfront as Small Robert due to his short height, and that Northern journalists transmuted this into the name he would later use as a Congressman and power broker in Republican National Conventions.)

Here Smalls stood as a slave. He could see the masts and stacks of the Federal blockade fleet (although not their hulls at that distance). It all looks so close when you see it in person, so immediately within reach. At least that giant, auto-transport ship looked surprisingly within reach as I sat there that afternoon.

Beside us, just to the north of the yacht club, is a mansion built on concrete piers out over the harbor. It was built by a software magnate on an old Navy degaussing station. The Navy pilings form what is now a long dock for his megayacht. The dock is lined with solar panels. Huger says the mansion's owner told him the solar panels generate so much electricity he sells the surplus back to the utility grid, after he has air-conditioned and lighted his over-the-water mansion, his guest house on shore, his long dock, and his plugged-in megayacht alongside it.

I normally keep my boat at the Cooper River Marina in North Charleston, on the old Navy base. To get to that marina, you have to drive through the impoverished, black neighborhood at the south end of North Charleston (not the gentrified, predominately white neighborhood a few blocks to the north.) In the black neighborhood, you must watch closely for pedestrians, particularly at night. Indolent men, mostly young, but some middle-aged, amble along the streets with their pants sagging ridiculously below their butts, their underwear exposed. They appear to be drunk or on drugs. On rare occasions, they clutch at young children, in what seems to be a pitiful moment of baby-daddy-longing to be a good father. But you can see these young men's future written clearly. Incarceration, drug addiction, alcoholism, early death. You see their women pushing the children in strollers. Could the children escape? Could they make it out? It's just a few miles away. Down to the East Battery.

Scholarly sources list that North Charleston neighborhood as one of the few surviving enclaves of Gullah/Geechee culture in the 21st Century.

We were four or five miles away from there, and a hell of a lot farther away than that, as we had cocktails moored to the Carolina Yacht Club transient dock.

The next morning, after we had strolled down Rainbow Row to a trendy bakery for coffee and scones, I took Tom and Mac to see the Smalls historical marker on the battery. The marker has only been there four or five years. When it was first placed, a marker to a Black Civil War hero erected in one of the most expensive and desirable neighborhoods in the United States, someone tore it down and vandalized it within a couple of months.

But it was re-erected, and there it stood for Tom and Mac to see. Tom read it and said he vaguely remembered Smalls's story from a television documentary in recent years. I first heard of Smalls by reading a Wikipedia article the previous fall. I grew up in South Carolina. I had to study South Carolina history twice as a boy. It was required, as I recall, in the third grade and again in the eighth in public schools. In the third grade, there were only white kids in my school. By the eighth grade, my class had black kids in it. I had a black history teacher in the seventh grade. He was the first black man I had ever known with a college degree. That year- 1970- schools in Spartanburg, South Carolina, were integrated by court order. That was sixteen years after the U.S. Supreme Court outlawed school segregation in *Brown Versus Board of Education*. Today, the schools in Spartanburg have been resegregated by two generations of people moving themselves into different neighborhoods, as the schools have been gradually resegregated over the past forty years in most school districts across the United States. But that is neither here nor there.

In the state-sanctioned study of South Carolina history of my youth, there was no mention of Robert Smalls. There was little mention of Reconstruction. That was far too seedy and dark a period of South Carolina history to teach to young children, I suppose. I studied Reconstruction in high school and college as a minor part of American history. You may remember Reconstruction. It was summed up in a brief scene in *Gone with the Wind*. Remember that scene? A carpetbag-toting white man and a fat black man (looking, by the way, remarkably like photographs of Congressman Robert Smalls), whip their way in a shiny carriage past the starving, noble Confederate soldiers making their way home from the war.

While I had studied the terrible misdeeds of Reconstruction governments as a brief chapter (or sub-chapter) of American history, I had never heard of Robert Smalls. I never heard of Robert Smalls until the fall of 2012. I was teaching at our community college in South Carolina. I had a student I found particularly likable and promising, a young, black man named Robert Lewson. Robert entered my life in an English 101 class for which he and so many of his fellows were hopelessly ill-prepared. I remember him at the beginning of the semester. He rolled in. How can I describe this ridiculous roll? He eyed the room, hoping someone would notice, or maybe he was hoping no one would notice. He was lost, utterly lost. The outfit was ridiculous. The flat-rimmed ball cap was tilted and cocked at a farcical angle. His hand, clutched at his private parts, held up baggy designer jeans sagging below his ass in the back. His underwear clung to his bloated butt cheeks. His enormous, vinyl athletic shoes were untied. The entire appearance had taken quite some time to don and arrange at home in front of his mirror. It had cost more than all the clothes I would wear to class in a week. I wondered how its precarious positioning had been maintained in the car or bus ride out to the Community College campus, not to mention the stroll across campus in that August heat.

There was nothing remarkable in Bobby Lewson's entrance to the world of higher education. I meet a dozen Bobby Lewsons every semester. I have learned how to overcome their stance of resistance. I have learned how to get them to believe, if only for a moment, that they might succeed at college and escape from the dead-end world of drugs and violence, incarceration and early death to which American society condemns them. I have watched a few- a very few- actually finish the semester and complete the course. I have rarely seen one of these young men, though, walk across the stage at graduation. I have seen black men walk across the stage, but they are different. They don't dress like this. They don't walk like this. They don't talk like this.

I have always been on the side of the Bobby Lewsons in the classroom. I keep on hoping, I guess, but I've learned not to get my hopes too high.

In that particular class, after the initial weeks, Bobby sort of caught on fire. The others in the class considered him a ridiculous clown. But I listened to Bobby. I soon knew he was smart. I soon knew he was terrifically dyslexic.

Bobby caught fire on an essay about Faulkner's "A Rose for Emily." Bobby pointed out Emily's black servant Tobe is entirely silent throughout the story. Bobby said that silence portrayed the plight of African Americans not only in Faulkner's society, but in American society as a whole. Continuing his argument, he said

Tobe would have been entirely deprived of political power in his lifetime.

I thought Bobby would be interested to learn that Tobe, in fact, had not been deprived of political power during his entire lifetime. In Tobe's younger years, during Reconstruction, African-Americans were in fact transcendent in their political power in Mississippi. To help Bobby see that, I Googled up Wikipedia articles on a few Reconstruction-era, black office-holders in Mississippi and pasted the links in my comments to him. The articles were fascinating to me. So I Googled up Wikipedia articles on South Carolina's black office-holders from Reconstruction, and then I found Robert Smalls.

What a guy! Robert Smalls, that is. Why had I never heard of him? He had been expunged from history- that's why! He had been deliberately and systematically expunged from history.

Later, I asked a friend who currently teaches eighth-grade South Carolina history if she were familiar with Smalls. She was, I was delighted to learn. Smalls has been resurrected in recent years, which was why my friend Tom had seen a television show on him, although he couldn't really recall Smalls's name.

I'm dropping my discussion of Robert Lewson, by the way, not because he is neither here nor there. Bobby is very here and very there. He is everywhere for me. But I can't really talk about Bobby right now. Maybe later.

That morning, after the tide turned, we cast off from the yacht club and sailed through the harbor, past Castle Pinckney and Fort

Sumter and Fort Moultrie on Sullivan's Island, and past the shallow part of the harbor where Fort Wagner once stood.

When we got offshore, we turned south and had the most lovely beam reach, in gentle two-to-four-foot swells, along the coast of Morris Island and Folly Island. We sailed past Stono Inlet, which is still impassable without intimate local knowledge, and sailed into North Edisto Inlet. We ran up the North Edisto River in a late-afternoon sea breeze and turned up Steamboat Creek to anchor at a place called Steamboat Landing.

The May air was cool as we anchored The sun was settling over a vast expanse of marshgrass to the North and East. Forested islands rose here and there. We put the outboard on the dinghy and motored ashore at the small public landing. From there, we walked down a sandy road toward the interior of Edisto Island. The heat rose as we moved inland, and mosquitoes oscillated in slanted afternoon sunlight. The road became a dark tunnel bored through live oaks, Spanish moss, and scrub Palmetto understory. The tree frogs and birds sang their other-worldly cadence.

Tom and Mac were uncomfortable in this unfamiliar setting, so different from the Caribbean charter-boat experience. The water was murky. It was hot and humid. There was the black, sticky marsh mud.

We dinghied back to the boat that evening. After many drinks, I cooked my friends a dinner of shrimp and grits. A pod of dolphins lolled on the creek surface around us as the tide began to flow in, and the sun settled spectacularly over green salt marsh and the pine islands scattered in it. As the sun set, no-seeums attacked. We spread mosquito nets to keep them out of the cockpit.

And as the evening wore on and we emptied another bottle of wine, we talked as old college friends will do. We were still the closest of friends, having passed through marriages made and destroyed and children loved and hurt and careers made and lost and hearts broken and despair survived and joy transporting. We began to muse in the star-filled night, as the tree frogs sang from the live oaks on shore, their song drifting over that salt marsh in the sea breeze, and the dolphins blew in the darkness here and there beside us in the creek. We talked of the tide-like movements of our lives. We talked of the nature of the universe.

I said I thought the universe was in fact organized upon and motivated by grace, and that we were simply blind to that reality for much of our lives. We think the universe and our lives in it are so often terrifying, or desperate, or without direction, I said, but through it all there is grace providing all we need, more than we need, really, taking these three far-flung, college friends, senior citizens now, and putting them on a sailboat in this place with the dolphins and the tree-frogs singing to us.

I pointed out an argument made by Ghandi, in his book *Indian Home Rule*, written when Indian home rule was just Ghandi's dream. Critics of Ghandi's non-violent approach claimed it was doomed to defeat in a world dominated by violence. Ghandi said history definitively disproved their objection. If non-violence and peaceful coexistence were not, in fact, the ultimate organizing principles of human society, he said, human beings would surely no longer exist. Their love of warfare, violence, and cruelty would have destroyed them all long ago.

Similarly, I said, if grace and mercy and hope were not the organizing forces of the universe, we would not be in this setting on Steamboat Creek, sung to by the forest spirits of Edisto Island and the dolphin spirits in the muddy creek waters, lit by the numberless stars of heaven. The despair, heartbreak, and chaos of our lives would have long ago done us in.

Tom and Mac liked that. They said so. We sat in silence in the cockpit for a while, and we drank more wine.

The next morning was clear and unseasonably cool, without a cloud in a deep blue sky. We all had a considerable hangover. I was consulting the charts on the computer to plan the next leg south. I noticed again the name of the creek where we were anchored- Steamboat Creek- and the name of that place- Steamboat Landing. I don't know why it had never occurred to me before.

Suddenly I realized that was where people came to Edisto in the centuries before a highway bridge connected the island to the mainland. This was the place the steamboat landed, and almost everyone who ever came and went from Edisto in centuries past must have gone through that very place where we had found ourselves in the night.

The Dreamer

We loaded barrels of salt pork, flour, and beans aboard the *Planter* at the steamboat landing on Edisto Island and headed down the creek with the tide, our ship ably piloted by none other than the famous Robert Smalls, who had commandeered this very vessel from under the noses of the Confederates in Charleston harbor. What better example of the courage and ingenuity of the colored race? My experience of the past few weeks had offered little to contradict my belief in these freed coloreds' abilities and potential. They were as fine a lot of soldiers as I had ever seen.

We steamed down the North Edisto River, through a landscape quite foreign. The river was wide, with expanses of green marsh grass spreading along the banks for miles. Beyond were deeply forested islands, only occasionally punctuated by a glimpse of a plantation house or outbuilding.

Moving across the water in the light breeze gave some relief from the oppressive, July heat. Boston can be stifling this time of the year, but there was something inescapable and crushing about this heat. The heavy humidity, the high angle of the sun, the incessant assault of blood-sucking insects, and the heavy wool of our uniforms were overwhelming.

We had a short run north up the coast to Stono Inlet and Folly Island, where the 54th was encamped, and where our supplies were quickly disembarked and delivered. Our camp was exotic there. White canvas tents ranged in perfectly straight files among the palm trees. The dunes were covered in waving sea oats. And there the black-faced troops drilled under the review of Colonel Shaw, their weeks of training in Massachusetts showing in the sharp precision of their movements.

Anticipation of action filled the air. An assault on Fort Wagner just to our north had failed a few days earlier. We had heard the roar of the battle, a few miles distant, with a mixture of delight and dread. We officers, all battle-hardened now after more than two years of war, knew well what we were missing. The sea breeze blew gently over us among the sand dunes. The troops wore the confused and pensive expressions of green troops on the cusp of battle. Though these were the best men selected from an overabundance of black volunteers, now that we were in the field the reality of what they had gotten themselves into was becoming clearer.

Some three days after I delivered supplies from Edisto Island, we were ordered to move north for another assault on Fort Wagner. After marching up the sandy, narrow island, we were ferried across the swift current of the inlet in small boats and took up our positions in trenches besieging the fort.

Fort Wagner was not an impressive sight. There was a palisade of sharpened palmetto logs ringing it, almost like a frontier fort in the wilderness. Behind that the sand had been piled into mounds some fifteen or twenty feet high, in the angular arrangement of a masonry fort. But the effects of wind and bombardment had rounded these walls into something resembling tall sand dunes. We could see the Confederates' flag and guns, and here and there the tops of their tents peeked over the dunes, but there was little else to take notice of from our position.

Between us and the fort, the island narrowed to a spit some sixty yards wide, squeezed in by ocean on the right and salt marsh on the left.

The bombardment started around noon. Six monitors closed within a quarter mile of the beach, and for the next seven or eight hours they unleashed a continual bombardment on the fort. Our guns on the left flank of our entrenchments joined relentlessly in the attack. There was no sign of the rebels. The shells exploded in their fort, spewing clouds of sand into the air. Over the course of the afternoon, the walls of the fort crumbled and spilled down their own slopes, like a sandcastle drying and crumbling in the sun. But what remained was still a high dune overlooking the palmetto palisade and the moat we would later find behind it.

After we spent an unbearably hot afternoon in the trenches watching this bombardment, the sun began to settle to our west over the marshes. I remember the beauty of that setting sun, crowning the anvil-shaped head of a thunderstorm in the distance. I don't know why that sight has stayed with me so during the years-looking down the trench at the faces of all those brave, black men, clutching their rifles, thinking the thoughts of men facing the terrible unknown, the most awful of fears, and above them, the sun sending forth a magnificent crown of rays among the towering storm clouds.

Colonel Shaw ordered us out of the trenches while it was still daylight. The 54th led the assault across that narrow isthmus, then pivoted to the left to attack the west wall of the fort. As our lines crowded into the isthmus, the brutal rebel firing commenced. I could see rebel troops massing now along the tops of the sand walls, emerging from the shelters where they had weathered the bombardment. Men began falling around me, their moment of heroism having lasted, in total, no more than a few minutes. The remaining brave troops pressed forward, notably more determined than any I had fought with before.

The rebel fire became intense as we pivoted to the west to begin our assault. We quickly were pinned down behind the palmetto log palisade. The hail of bullets and artillery was as terrible as any I ever encountered. It is difficult to remember this part of the battle. I think my mind, in an effort to heal itself, has erased much of this horror.

One isn't inclined to ruminate on warfare when one is in the midst of it, but in the years and decades that follow, one is haunted. There are two elements here: the memories of the men you knew in all their humanity, their strength, their fears, their weaknesses, their humors, their laughter. And then there is the memory of the slaughter by the buzzing bullets and exploding shells, the impaling on the sharpened spikes in the foul moat, the impaling (like Colonel Shaw) on the walls of the fort itself by rebel bayonets in the dark, that horrible, pitch-darkness of the night that fell, illuminated in flashing light that spewed from the rifle bores.

We fought to the top of that tall sand dune, the former sculpted wall of the fort. Then we tumbled in retreat back down it, across the moat, scrambling through the sand dunes, attempting to drag our wounded, being mown down by incessant fire. The screaming of the wounded and dying was horrible.

The heartbreak of this particular battle was the role I had played in recruiting these colored men to this fate. It had not been a hard sell. They wanted so desperately to fight for the freedom of their fellows in the South. They wanted so desperately to be fully considered as men.

One memory that plagues me was watching a group of half a dozen of our troops being taken prisoner along the top of the sand wall. I saw them with their hands held high as we scrambled back down the wall. I saw the rebels grab them roughly and throw them down into the darkness on the other side. I knew what awaited them. I had come to know these men. I had heard the stories of what so many of them had gone through to become free men in the

North. And now I had delivered them again into the hell they had fled.

We retreated pell-mell across the isthmus and took to our trenches again. The firing stopped. The whole vicious fight had taken place in no more than a couple of hours, most of it in darkness, lit by cannon fire, rifle flash, and screaming rockets. Fort Wagner remained in rebel hands, still blocking our approaches to Charleston.

The next day, the rebels buried piles of corpses in front of the fort. It is not too much to say they buried a thousand bodies in one long, shallow, sand pit.

Over the next two months, our constant bombardment unearthed these rotting hordes of the dead. We watched them tumbling through the air, whole or in pieces, along with the sand spewing from each explosion.

By September, the stench had become so unbearable the rebels were forced to abandon their position. They evacuated Fort Wagner by boat in the dark of night. We moved in, buried the foul remains as best we could, rebuilt the rebel fortifications, and began our bombardment of Charleston.

The White Officer

After Smalls delivered the *Planter* to the U.S. Navy, it was billeted over to the Army. It was a wood-burner, and Navy vessels · ran on coal. The Navy had no capability to supply fuel for a wood-burner. Also, the boat was far better suited for moving supplies and troops up and down the rivers and creeks of South Carolina. As large and commodious as she was, the *Planter* only drew a bit over three feet, so we could run in and out among the sand bars and shifting channels with ease. But she was top heavy and rolly at sea.

Smalls knew the local waters remarkably well. The fellow couldn't read a lick, though he studied our charts earnestly and seriously. Eventually he learned to recognize numbers and seemed to be able to read soundings and bearings. But he really didn't need those. He knew the necessary bearings and soundings on these waters better than any U.S. Navy chart would show them.

The resupply of Morris Island had always been a problem. Landing small boats on the ocean beach was impossible in all but the calmest of weather. The inlet likewise was unapproachable from the sea with any sort of swell running. So supplies for our sizable garrison there, along with ammunition for the heavy guns that were shelling Charleston and Fort Sumter, had to be offloaded on Folly Island, dragged by wagon along the miring sand tracks of that island, reloaded on to small boats, and rowed across the inlet to Morris.

Smalls came up with the idea to resupply Morris by running the creeks on the inside. Folly Creek runs fairly deep and wide for several miles, winding inland toward Confederate lines at Secessionville. Smalls felt by taking a couple of creeks that branched off to the east, he could pilot *Planter* through at high tide and steam down to the inlet between Morris and Folly. Scouts were sent one night to sound the passage in small boats. They found the plan viable.

We got underway two days later with a cargo of supplies. We steamed up Folly Creek in broad daylight, winding left and right though the marsh, closer and closer to the Confederate batteries at Secessionville. By the time those batteries started firing, we were well within their range, and the *Planter* began taking hits immediately.

Within minutes, it was clear we were trapped. Folly Creek at that point was too narrow for us to turn around. The *Planter* could not back down the stream against the flood current. She couldn't be steered in reverse. The flood current was carrying us closer to the guns at Secessionville. We were taking furious fire, and the *Planter* did not have enough armor to withstand the onslaught.

Captain Nickerson had no choice. He called me to the wheelhouse and gave the order to strike colors and raise a white flag. The strain and dismay on his face were remarkable, but I knew it was the right thing to do. Continuing up the river would quickly result in the destruction of the *Planter* and unnecessary loss of life. Neither of us wanted to become a prisoner of war, but that was the only choice other than certain death, and I felt the Captain was doing his duty.

I had failed to bring Robert Smalls into my calculations.

Smalls loudly demanded that I ignore the captain's order. I looked at him, I'm sure, with utter astonishment, as projectiles from Confederate guns crashed into the ship and the surrounding marsh. Smalls had the steamer moving at flank speed. He could hardly take his eyes away from the water in front of the ship, the tidal creek was so tight and twisting.

Several of his colored crewmen gathered around the wheelhouse. Smalls loudly explained to the Captain that, while we, the white crew members, risked little in surrendering, he and the other coloreds faced execution at the hands of the Rebels for stealing the *Planter*. They could not, under any circumstances, surrender, he told the Captain.

The Captain reacted with astonishment and growing rage. The ship was shattered by cannonballs. Exploding shells burst around us, spewing shrapnel. The *Planter* continued at flank speed up the river.

The Captain ordered Smalls to stop the ship. Smalls did not react. The Captain ordered me again to strike colors and hoist a flag of surrender. Smalls told me, in the most commanding of voices, not to do so.

I hesitated. Smalls acted. He ordered the other coloreds to take the Captain below and lock him in the wood hold. They did not hesitate.

The Captain was led below. I stood on the deck of the wheelhouse, staring at the marsh speeding past us and the shells as they exploded. Smalls steered the ship with determined ire. I realized I had allowed a mutiny on a United States ship of war. I must act to stop it, I knew.

But I could not. Smalls was no longer the colored pilot of that ship, a civilian in the service of the U.S. Army. He had, in the space of a couple of minutes, become the commander of the thing, and I was unable to react in any appropriate way.

I've long wondered about that moment. After years of reflection, it occurs to me that much of our life is dependent on knowing our place. Each of us has a role to play. We are a son, a brother, a father, a citizen, a soldier, an officer, an enlisted man, a servant, a master.... In almost any interaction with any other human being, we must know our place in order to function.

Abraham Lincoln was born in a log cabin and became President. But President Lincoln did not simply walk into the White House one day and start acting like the President. He followed an order of progression. He occupied the correct sequence of places as he moved up to his ultimate position.

Robert Smalls had no sense of how one could or should do this. Smalls simply was. He simply stepped into the moment and took the action that was needed. This was a magnificent thing to watch. But it was terrifying and disconcerting to those around him.

The ship steamed up the river under ferocious fire, now, sustaining heavier and heavier damage. Smalls was determined, calm, concentrated at the wheel. Suddenly, he turned sharply to starboard, into one of the narrow creeks headed east. I expected at any moment to run aground and be left entirely at the mercy of the rebel bombardment, but Smalls kept the ship moving at flank speed.

I stood a coward, sweating, shaking, expecting my life as an officer was finished, expecting incarceration at best, execution at worst. Within minutes, Smalls had steamed out of range of the guns. The shells spewed up water, marsh grass, and mud behind us, and then they went silent. Smalls piloted the *Planter* down the creek to the inlet at Morris Island.

My confusion in the ensuing days was intense, but I retained a sense of how the Army was structured, and the coward in me navigated quite effectively through that structure. Captain Nickerson, released from the wood-hold upon our arrival at Morris Island, was immediately relieved of command. Robert Smalls was appointed captain of the *Planter*, and as such, lays claim to being the first colored captain of a United States ship of war. Nickerson was later court-martialed for cowardice under fire.

I, the real coward in the incident, had, by virtue of my inaction, taken the side of the victor. I retained my commission and continued my advance through the ranks for the rest of the war.

Uncle Romulus

Robert Smalls used this incident for the rest of his life to try to get money from the Federal Government. And his political enemies used it to deny him money from the Federal Government. Was he a Navy Captain? He surely had all the duties of a Navy Captain for the rest of the war. Was he entitled to a Navy Captain's pension? As a civilian captain of a U.S. Army ship, no, his opponents argued. When he was a U.S. Congressman, and even in the years after his service in Congress, Smalls put forth much effort trying to get money out of the U.S. Government. Was this because he was a venal, vain man, or was it because he was just trying to get his fair share of what was due him?

I know venal. I know vain. I know trying to get my fair share.

You do, too.

I've already mentioned my bankruptcy and my brief sojourn in a mental hospital, but I haven't really gone there with you. Perhaps I should go there with you now.

When I went broke, my wife left. She left on the occasion of our twenty-fifth wedding anniversary. She walked out as I was planning a weekend trip to a friend's lake house to celebrate. We didn't have money to do anything else.

Why did she stop loving me? Maybe the question should be, why did I think she had stopped loving me? She was facing a mess, a man who had defined himself in terms that were meaningless and empty. Now he was faced with the reality of that pitiful waste of his life. And she had spent her life with him. I don't wonder, now, why she ran.

At the time I saw none of this. I was frantic. I was irrational. My wife fled to her sister's house out of town. Like a stalker, I called and emailed. She told me to stop trying to communicate with her.

She made me promise to stop contacting her. I was left alone.

In the night, in the long, dark, solitary night that followed, it became clear to me. I needed to kill myself.

It became crystal clear. I needed to pull down the attic door. I needed to go upstairs and take my Browning 12-gauge from its leather case. I needed to climb back down the attic stairs. I needed to go into one of my daughters' bedrooms, where I kept a couple of boxes of ammunition from an old dove hunt.

I needed to take the ammunition and the gun and walk out to the front yard. I needed to slide a shell into the chamber. I needed to put the muzzle of the twelve gauge in my mouth and blow the top of my head off.

It would blow off just like the top of my sister's head. My corpse would look just like the corpse Grace found when she discovered her mother's suicide- its head exploded like a huge jelly donut- a grotesque face draped on one side.

I needed to do this in the front yard, so my neighbors would see and hear it. They would then call the police. The police would retrieve the body and hide the hideous mess long before my wife or any of my daughters could get there. This would relieve my loved ones of further suffering. This would end the decades of misery. This was the thing to do. It was the only thing to do.

I prayed fervently. I prayed the hardest and longest and most heated and most sincere prayer of all my life. I begged. Please help me, Jesus! Please help me! I prayed and prayed and cried and begged and talked to Jesus.

This brought silence.

He did not answer.

There was silence.

He would not come.

I got out of bed. I walked into the hallway.

I stood underneath the attic door.

I reached up and grabbed the pull cord.

I stood there, for the longest time. I stood there, shaking and crying.

I prayed and prayed.

There was no answer. None that I could hear.

I pulled down the attic door.

I unfolded the attic stairs. It was hard for me to move. My limbs felt like lead.

I climbed the attic stairs.

I pulled the string to turn on the light.

Six feet in front of me, on the plywood floor, lay my shotgun. It was in a leather case I had since college. The case was old and torn.

I unzipped the end of the case and pulled the stock of the gun toward me. It was made of oiled walnut. It was scratched with age. The grip was checked with a fine, familiar pattern. I held it in my palm. The barrel and muzzle were still in the case.

I had bought this gun at a pawnshop when I was a kid. It was a Belgium-made, Browning 12-gauge. I had hunted with it my whole life.

I smelled gun oil.

I felt the checked grip and the cold trigger. I was reminded of many, many mornings duck hunting in an old rice field on the Combahee River.

We stood loin-deep in the cold, dark water, hidden in the reeds. We heard mallards quacking above us in the dawn fog, but we could not see them. I quacked back to them. I talked to them in their magical, quacking language, and they quacked to me.

And I could hear their wings whistling in the fog, as the ducks tucked their wings into that beautiful arc which carries them down from the heavens. I could hear their arced wings whistling until the birds appeared in front of us, twisting and bobbing to settle into the decoys.

After a long time- after a long, long time- for some reason, for some reason I don't understand, I let go of my gun. I set it down, still halfway inserted in its case. I climbed back down the attic stairs.

I left the stairs unfolded and the attic door open.

I walked to the other end of the house. There I sat at the computer and Googled, "How not to commit suicide."

The web page that appeared counseled procrastination. Procrastination was the key, it said. Just keep putting it off minute by minute. Put it off until you can be with someone else.

It was around four in the morning. I knew my neighbor across the street would wake up around six o'clock to prepare for work.

I sat at the window in the computer room and watched the blacked out windows across the street. I watched until six o'clock, when the first light went on at my neighbor's house.

Then I crossed the street in my pajamas and bare feet. I rang my neighbor's doorbell. And I told him what was going on.

Later that day, I was hospitalized. The doctors diagnosed me with General Anxiety Disorder. I am too afraid.

The British Mariner

I have long felt that there is a special hatred for the Negro in the American. Why this should be, I have never fathomed. The poor Negroes are so beaten down, so broken, you would think the whites would pity rather than despise them. Why would one not despise the plutocrat and feel compassion for the downtrodden? But this is distinctly not the American way. The average American, unlettered, rough-hewn, and rough-mannered as he is, thinks of his wealthy oppressor as his friend and hero. The poor man he thinks of as a problem, and the lowly Negro is a thing to be feared, despised, and humiliated at every opportunity. This is as much a part of American culture as the Fourth of July. It is perhaps a defining component of American culture. The Indian must be exterminated. The Chinaman is a subhuman that must be exploited. But they have a special hatred for the Negro.

That hatred manifests itself in the cataclysm of self-destruction in which they now find themselves embroiled. What is that war but a fight over their black men? The Southerners want to keep the poor creatures in their pitiful condition of chattel servitude. The Northerners, angry at the fight, riot against the draft in New York City and attack poor Negroes on the street as the cause of the conflict.

Missionaries flock to Port Royal, to educate and convert the Negroes, one imagines, into prim New Englanders, to turn them into dark-skinned, white people. Nowhere is there the concept that these are already fully-formed, human beings, with their own language, culture, music, art, and family structure. I have never yet met the white American who can look a black man in the eye as his equal and fellow citizen. And Robert Smalls, who is so clearly the superior of most men around him, leaves the American white man as disoriented as a landlubber in a Grand Banks fog.

So it took a while, I suppose, for Smalls's fellow officers to compose themselves and react to his sudden elevation. At first, they dressed him in a Captain's uniform and afforded him all the rights and privileges of that rank. But this could not last long. They could not salute a black man without cringing. It only took a few weeks before they started talking among themselves about his comeuppance. They muttered secretly at first. Later, it became a matter of regular conversation in the public houses of Beaufort, a conversation held openly, if in low voices, among all white speakers.

When the colored servants approached, the subject was dropped. But the coloreds, who worshiped Smalls, knew what was happening.

The order was cooked up for Smalls to take the *Planter* to Philadelphia Naval Shipyard for refitting. Everyone knew Smalls was illiterate. He knew the waters of South Carolina and Georgia better than any Navy cartographer had ever surveyed them. But he could not read a chart, could not begin to handle a sextant or compute a sight, and the thought of his navigating from South Carolina to Philadelphia was absurd.

The *Planter* herself was not suited for the voyage. Her low free board, shallow draft, wide beam, and top-heavy house would make her a death trap in a Hatteras gale. The mission was a suicide run. It is difficult to believe no one up the chain of command had the decency to belay the order.

Smalls, by far one of the cleverest men I've ever known, was fully aware what they were doing to him. In his situation, I'm not sure what I would have done. It would be one thing if my fellows were plotting my potential death. It would be another if they were willing to sacrifice two dozen of my crewmen in the bargain. I don't know how Smalls contained his ire. But he did. He took the order as if they had told him to ferry a load of troops up the coast to Georgetown. And then he came to me.

I was amazed at his request. He had three weeks to prepare for the voyage, three weeks in which he had also to fulfill his normal duties of command. He wanted me to teach him all he would need to know to navigate the *Planter* to Philadelphia. I was at a loss how to teach him what he needed to know in that period of time. And he insisted, quite rightly, that we keep our lessons confidential.

Yet within three weeks, Smalls was as able a navigator as any green lieutenant emerging from the naval academy. He could reduce a sight with confidence, working his way through the tables and computing the lines of position with surprising accuracy. We were only able to practice his use of the sextant from the steady deck of his ship anchored in the Beaufort River, and I'm sure taking real sights at sea posed some difficulty for him, as it does any novice navigator.

He had years of experience as a coastal pilot behind him, and I learned a thing or two from teaching him. In no time, he had memorized the coastline all the way to Long Island, poring over the charts as if he were surveying the forested shore. He couldn't read the names of the capes and towns and lights and islands, but he memorized them all. He asked what vegetation the shore had, what elevation it had. He studied the pictures of the lighthouses in the light list until he could identify each one by its paint patterns. He asked about the color of the water, its depth, the currents, and the way the sea rose and fell in which wind patterns at each location. The man thought of the sea in ways I never had, although as he questioned me, I realized I knew the route myself in much the same way, as many times as I had traveled it.

Robert knew the sea as well as a shore person knows the landscape of their home county, so that he could look out upon a familiar seascape with no land on the horizon and know where he was. By questioning me in this unexpected way, he quickly learned the sea from Charleston to Delaware Bay nearly as well.

I was not surprised to hear the *Planter* hailed a pilot off of the entrance to Delaware Bay three days after its departure from Port Royal, having encountered nothing untoward in her voyage up that treacherous, war-torn coast.

Uncle Romulus

Jacob, a tenured professor at the University of Virginia, is a well-respected authority on Abraham Lincoln. Jacob is one of my sailing buddies. He usually takes a week off in the summer to go sailing with me. This summer, he joined me in Charleston for a cruise down the coast of South Carolina.

When I told Jacob I was working on a book about Robert Smalls, he was enthralled. He vaguely remembered hearing or reading Smalls's story, but he couldn't recall much beyond the ship-stealing and some role in Reconstruction. I gave a thumbnail sketch of Smalls's life. I told of Smalls's meeting with Lincoln, which influenced Lincoln to allow Negroes to enlist in the army. "You know it's amusing," Jacob said, "how after Lincoln's assassination, all sorts of people claimed to have met with him and influenced him in making some historic decision."

Well, I was deflated. I knew I had read about the Smalls/Lincoln meeting in several historical sources. There was clear consensus that General Hunter sent Smalls to Washington, accompanied by Reverend Mansfield French, on a mission to convince Lincoln to allow black troops to enlist in the U.S. Army. There was clear consensus, I thought, that Smalls had met first with Secretary of War Stanton, and then with Lincoln, and that this mission had led directly to the desired change of policy.

But, for goodness' sake, here was one of the leading Lincoln scholars in the country. He had barely even heard of Smalls.

At least until now. For the next three days, as we sailed through the landscape at the heart of the Smalls story, Jacob pumped me for details and delighted in the enormous irony and poignancy of Smalls's life. We cruised down the Stono River, to the inlet where Smalls had led the Union invaders, and we anchored there. I pointed out the islet where the Confederates had abandoned their fort. I pointed out the location of their batteries at Secessionville, far in the distance over the marshes.

We couldn't go out the inlet, of course, because it is so treacherous, so we motored back up the Stono, intending to take the Intracoastal Waterway south toward Beaufort. After less than half an hour of running, the exhaust elbow on our diesel engine blew out, spewing exhaust and cooling water into the cockpit locker. We had to abandon our cruise plans.

Back in the marina, we took the blown-out part to a welder, left it to be repaired, and faced a couple of days of unplanned vacation. Jacob Googled up a touring museum exhibition entitled: "The Life and Times of Congressman Robert Smalls," which was open for one more week at the church in Beaufort where Smalls was buried. It was Jacob's idea to drive down there that afternoon.

We left after lunch, drove to Beaufort (about an hour away) and found the Tabernacle Baptist Church, where Smalls is buried. Here the only public monument to him is erected, and here the touring exhibit was on display. A middle-aged, African-American woman was seated in the foyer as docent. She was doing a find-the-word puzzle. We were the only visitors.

Most of the material was new to Jacob. But much of it was rather superficial, and I had already studied far deeper into Smalls's story. For instance, a panel early in the exhibition said Henry McKee was widely believed to be Smalls's father. This belief was long widely-held, but recent biographers have cast a great deal of doubt. First, I told Jacob, look at this photo of Smalls and this photo of McKee. See any resemblance?

Jacob could see no resemblance. McKee was a slender, grizzled, white man. Robert Smalls was a plump, dark-skinned, African-looking man. There was no similarity in the faces.

"And this person," I said (pointing to a drawing of Smalls's mother, Lydia), "raised Henry McKee as his slave mammy. She was much older than Henry. She was in her forties when Robert was born. It's quite a stretch to imagine her having an affair with Henry.

It would almost be like sleeping with her own child." After my brief explanation, Jacob bought into my skepticism.

As we turned the corner into the next small room, I saw something I hadn't seen before. There was a shadow box with two bronze medallions on leather cords. The exhibit explained these were medallions worn by slaves in Charleston, who, like Smalls, were hired out to work somewhere off their master's premises. Smalls would have been required to wear one of these medallions in public himself.

The medallions were stark. There was a three-digit number and then a word describing the work the slave was authorized to do. In these two cases: "Porter" and "Carpenter." No name was given.

I had read about this medallion system. Even free Negroes in pre-war Charleston were required to wear such medallions in public. But reading about the medallions doesn't do them justice. When you see them it hits you pretty hard- the number, the occupation, the knotted leather cord, and no other mark to show they might belong to a human being, a possessor of a soul.

"God," Jacob said. He turned to whisper to me, even though only the docent could have heard, "That looks like something out of Nazi Germany."

I had been thinking the same.

Smalls's medallion, which was not in the exhibit, would have said, "Wheelman", I suppose. Though he was a skilled and widely recognized pilot, slaves couldn't be called pilots. He would have been a wheelman.

In the next room, we saw Smalls's gold-handled walking cane. This was a post-war artifact of Senator Smalls, Congressman Smalls, General Smalls, the King of Beaufort County.

"He beat the shit out of a white guy with this cane you know," I said.

Jacob laughed.

"He was walking down the street in Beaufort, and a white guy came out of the liquor store and called him a 'nigger'. And Smalls beat the shit out of him, right there on the street. Smalls wore this big signet ring." I held out my hand to indicate where he would have worn it. "He turned the heavy part of the ring in toward his palm, and he slapped the guy up side the head, then he beat the shit out of him with his cane.

"The *Charleston Courier* ran an article on it, saying it was an example of how badly things were out of control in Reconstruction. They said Smalls was rumored to walk around the streets of Beaufort armed with a pistol."

There was a small, flat-screened television in the corner of that room. The docent started the movie for us. It was the PBS documentary done on Smalls, narrated by Morgan Freeman.

The documentary featured some reenactment footage (low production value) interspersed with interviews of historians, most of whom I recognized from my research. One of the historians, an African-American, said at the beginning of the Civil War Lincoln really wasn't focused at all on freeing slaves. In Lincoln's mind at that point, he said, the sole purpose of the war was to preserve the Union.

This irritated Jacob. He felt it unfairly characterized Lincoln's views on slavery.

We finished watching the movie. The director had abandoned Robert Smalls's story by the end of the film in order to frame a broader discussion of Reconstruction. Jacob didn't like that. He wanted to know more about Smalls. So did I.

Elsewhere in the exhibit was a looseleaf binder with photocopies of Smalls's hand-written letters to American presidents, politicians, and African-American leaders, including Frederick Douglass and Booker T. Washington. I had read some of Smalls's letters before. It's nice to hear someone speak for himself. There were two distinct hands in the letters. I assume the neater, more ordered hand belonged to Smalls's daughter, Elizabeth, who was educated at West Newton boarding school in Massachusetts She served as his secretary while he was in Congress.

The most interesting thing in the room was a panel displaying three *Boston Globe* columns from later in the 1800's, all about Smalls. They got harsher as time went by, and by 1889, the *Globe* reported on the outrage of that scalawag, thief, con man, and ruffian, "General Smalls", of Beaufort, who aroused open opprobrium from citizens on the streets of that town. Even now, the *Globe* reported, after his utter disgrace, Smalls had comfortably ensconced himself as the Chief Customs Inspector of Port Royal with a Federal salary.

Jacob and I loved the newspaper columns. We chuckled over them.

In the final small room of the exhibit, there were a few pieces of furniture belonging to Smalls, photographs of family members in the generations since he lived (I had seen all these before), and a photo of the U.S. Army transport ship that had been named for him in recent decades.

We walked onto the porch and asked the docent where Smalls was buried. She stuck her head over the porch rail and pointed a few feet in front of us. "Somewhere right in there," she said.

Indeed, there he lay, not twenty feet in front of us, between his wives. In the courtyard was a bronze bust of him, the only monument in existence, although others have recently been planned. In photographs, I had always thought this bust with its wavy, white-man's hair looked more like Mark Twain than Robert Smalls. But in person, the facial features are more strongly African, to the point of exaggeration, and I was less frustrated with it.

We left the church and walked toward Smalls's house. We talked about the exhibit and especially about *The Boston Globe* articles. The neighborhood of historic, clapboard houses, completely shaded by live oaks, was quaint, lovely, and humid. Beside the 18th-Century synagogue, just beside the old stucco arsenal, with its faux-medieval ramparts, we turned to the left.

I said the *Globe* was obviously a Democratic paper, and Jacob laughed. "Yeh," he said, "that's the way it was in 19th-Century America. Journalism was basically telling a good story. Reporters just made their stuff up to please their editors and their audiences. You can read two articles from two different papers about the same event, and you wonder if the two reporters were even in the same place at the same time. The accounts might have virtually nothing in common."

We walked a few short blocks, turned right on Prince Street, crossed the main drag, and found Smalls's house a couple of blocks ahead. It is in private hands, and it has an historical marker on the brick column beside the entry gate. It is a stately home, surrounded by over an acre of lush, elegantly landscaped gardens. Shaded porches run the width of the house on the first and second stories.

I had seen a video tour of the house a real estate agent posted on the Internet. He made extensive mention of the home's historic, Southern charm and its up-to-date, 21st-Century kitchen. He gave brief mention to Smalls, mainly to explain away the antique photographs of black people hanging in an upstairs hallway. It was an awkward moment for a South Carolina real estate agent showing a million-dollar home.

Jacob and I turned toward the waterfront, walked past the First African Baptist Church, and passed many other million-dollar homes before we got to the river. On the river-front we found a restaurant with a terrace where we could order a beer.

Jacob was intrigued by the museum exhibit. I knew, of course, that he knew far more about the period than I ever would.

There was a question I wanted to raise. I wanted to know what Lincoln thought of black people.

Jacob was thrilled when I asked. He led with the fact that Lincoln was the first U.S. President ever to meet with black men in the White House who were not servants. It was, he said, a meeting with a group of free blacks from Washington and Philadelphia in

August of 1862. Lincoln asked these black men to lead an effort to resettle freed slaves in a new Central American colony. Lincoln made the case to these men, Jacob said, that blacks and whites could never hope to live together in free society in the the United States.

That threw me back a little.

I said that was strange, because so many of the historical sources I read said Lincoln met with Smalls in August of 1862, when Smalls convinced the President to allow blacks to enlist in the Army. Those two meetings- ostensibly occurring in the same month- seemed incongruous, I said.

Jacob was silent for a moment.

I pondered.

On the other hand, I pointed out, I noticed the museum exhibit only said Smalls met with Secretary of War Stanton. The exhibit did not mention a meeting with Lincoln.

"It's possible Smalls met with the President," Jacob said. "And it's possible he didn't. I can't tell you for sure. There were no records kept in the White House of who met with the president in those days. People would just show up and hang out waiting for a chance to meet with him. In fact, they would often camp out overnight in the hallway waiting for him, and he would step over the bodies of these people as he made his way to his own bedroom in the evening.

"And consider this," Jacob said. "After he was assassinated, all of a sudden Lincoln was a saint. His popularity soared, and everyone wanted a piece of him. So people would tell their local paper about the time they met with him. The papers, who never fact-checked anything, would report the meeting, and then you've got a primary historical source. So the meeting winds up in the historical literature as fact. Ultimately, there's just no sure way to tell... It's possible.

"Now, as to how Lincoln really felt about blacks-" Jacob continued, "he was quite progressive for his era. You know, in the final weeks of his life, Lincoln said some black men should eventually be allowed to vote, but only the ones who had fought in the war, in addition to, and this is a direct quote: 'some intelligent ones.'"

We both laughed.

"It sounds so outrageously racist to us today," he continued, "but it was really radical at the time, and, ultimately, this is one of the things that prompted John Wilkes Booth to act on his assassination plans. So even saying this much in public got Lincoln killed.

"You know," Jacob said, "there is a whole line of argument in academia today that the slaves really freed themselves in the Civil War. It's as if these people want to write Lincoln out of his role as the Emancipator. And the film at that exhibit came from that perspective, I felt. I don't buy it. They're just rewriting history."

"Well," I chimed in, "look at Smalls."

Jacob smiled, shrugged, and threw his upturned palms toward heaven.

We laughed, and drank our beer, and looked out underneath the live oaks and Spanish moss, across the Beaufort River. In the midsummer heat, the river was bounded by bright, green marsh grass and black mud. The sea breeze blew our hair and cooled us a bit.

The Denizen

I read in the Enquirer this morning that Captain Smalls, the famous Negro who stole his ship from the Confederates in Charleston, was ejected from a streetcar on his way into town from the Philadelphia Naval Yard. The conductor of the streetcar claims he was simply enforcing the city's ordinances, which forbid Negroes riding on a public conveyance. The man was just doing his job, then, and the question, I suppose, is whether the ordinance itself is ill-advised and should be reformed.

Philadelphia, less than fifty miles from the Mason-Dixon line, is a haven for runaway Negroes. The city has had a large population of these people throughout my lifetime, and we find their ranks swelling since the war broke out. We encounter Negroes now throughout our day, and the city probably could not function in its current state without their labor as cooks, maids, stewards, delivery boys, gardeners, and so forth.

One encounters the occasional Negro such as Captain Smalls. The shop owner, the..., well, you get my point. Such individuals are a rarity in their race, and must we upset the natural order of society to make room for the rare exception?

I have not had the pleasure of meeting Captain Smalls. One hopes, as his ship is scheduled to be in the shipyard for several months, he may yet find his way into a drawing room where we could make his acquaintance. I understand he cuts quite the figure, articulate and charming. His reputation is so much more attractive than some of the abolitionist, radical Negroes. He is, after all, a warrior in a time of war.

Here is the point. What in the world will we do with all these Negroes if they are, indeed, freed? One feels the time is coming. Will they then all choose to move to Philadelphia? Will there be entire neighborhoods taken over by them? Will there be schools full of Negro children? Will there be gangs of Negro youth walking our streets, terrifying the populace?

And will there be more Negroes like Captain Smalls, engaged in activities hitherto reserved for those members of the better parts of society?

The possibilities make the head spin. The only reasonable solution, I think, will be to send these unfortunate creatures back to Africa. Perhaps there, the more intelligent ones, like Captain Smalls, carrying in him his father's white blood and abilities, could fashion a society based on democracy and education and law, carving out something of a modern nation in the wild jungles of their forebears.

In the meantime, if I were ever to set foot on a public streetcar, which, I confess, I am most unlikely ever to do, I would certainly not want to find sitting in front of me a Negro of any kind, even the well-dressed, well-mannered Captain Smalls. I'm just speaking plainly here. You have to draw the line somewhere. If we didn't draw lines, we couldn't function as a society. Let the public rancor swell, roar for a while, and then let it die down. If we change our ordinances about Negroes on public conveyances, we'll live to regret it.

The Planter

When Gennul Shumman done march to the sea is when them colored start pohin down outa countryside. They just walk off fum they owner and set theyseff free. The patrol done stop, and they wunt nothing to keep um slave, really, so they just walk off.

And mos of em come down roun top Beaufort, and down rown top Hilton Head and Port Royal and Savannah, cause people knowed that wuh where the colored wuh free and could join up the Army, and they wunt no Southern white folk to laud it oerm no mo.

That wuh when Gennul Shumman nounce he goin give evvy free colored famly forty acre and a mule. You aint hardly bleeb it now, the way they treat nigguhs roun here these day, lynching and whipping and murdering and cahyun on like they do. But I member it like it wuh yesterday. I tellin you boy. I live through it.

Yo ma and me, we join up with the ones goin get forty acres and a mule, and they put us on a steamship, the *Planter*, run by Gennul Bob Small. That brother wuh one fine, proud man. He a fine and a proud a any white man I ever see. He wuh Capn of that ship, and when we clamb on board he standin there at the gangplank, shakin our hand and talking Gullah to each and evuh brethren sister, tellin us welcome on board, we boun for black heaven. Black pahdice, he say. He laughin and smilin and cahyin on. I member that Bob Small I do.

And Capn Small he took us on that ship down in Jawjuh, up the Geechee river, and the yankee soldier, they wuh there at the landing, handin out paper and telling folk where to go to they new land. They give yo ma and me forty acre and a mule, and a wagon, and nuff vittel to lass six munt.

You aint never seed a place pretty a that farm. It wuh up on the marsh, overlooking the Geechee river, up on a bluff, and they wuh live oak all along, where we built our house, and the breeze blow up long that bluff all summuh long, where it aint hardly evuh hot in that house. And then out behind wuh the field. We had three big field of land, where yo ma reah chicken, and goat, and vejubble mo than we could eat, and then I reah cotton out yond all that.

And they wunt none of this lynchin and cahyun on back in them day. The yankee soldier wuh in charge, and the white men uh still off in the war, mos of em, and the one come back already wuh too beat up to do nothin to the colored back then.

I tell you what it wuh like, son. It wuh like the holy spirit done deliver us to the promise land. A man live he whole life, and he hear the preacher preachin and the women singin bout the Laud goin take care of him and whole him in he hand and the Laud done number the hair on he head. Well, for that two year, it wuh like that.

Coase it wunt real. They done kill President Lincoln, and President Johnson, he done take all that land back from the nigguh, and thowed us off, and we done walk back up to Beaufort on our bare feets.

And how we done get from that black heaven to this sorry state we in now, you ask, well it didn happen all twunce. It took a lifetime to get roun where it be nowday.

I member I got back to Beaufort, and yo ma just bout drag me off to chuch. I didn want no part of it. I done give up on hope and the Laud and the gumment and the yankee soldier. And she just drag me in to chuch with her one Sunday moaning, and they wuh Gennul Bob Small, come roun to talk to the brethren sister. And that man, he aint loss no hope. He wunt nothin but hope heseff. He say we goin build a black heaven right there in Beaufort County, what treat all the brethren sister, colored and white, like they the chillun of God they be.

That wuh a fine man, Bob Small. That wuh a fine a man as evuh be.

South of Broad

The final weeks of the war were a nightmare. I find it hard to recall. When I do, I shudder. After the Yankees occupied Fort Sumter, they began a continuous bombardment of downtown Charleston. The range of their guns ran nearly as high up the peninsula as Broad Street, and all the fine homes south of Broad were reduced to rubble. We relocated to Ansonborough, where we were safely out of range, and except for the noise, out of danger.

We were beaten, and we knew it, but the military men couldn't bring themselves to face the reality for several more weeks.

I remember the first Yankee soldiers marching up East Bay. The 54th Massachusetts was a phalanx of colored men in uniforms, as if they had taken all our servants and dressed them as soldiers, with white Yankee officers at the head of each company, marching up the street to drums and fifes, the Stars and Stripes flying in front of them.

Our slaves acted as if they had been transported. They ran into the streets, cheering and dancing and singing, as if we didn't even exist. We watched from upstairs windows. I had the most unexpected feeling of patriotism. I've never admitted this to anyone, of course, but for that brief moment, when the colored soldiers marched down East Bay with their white officers leading them, I felt the right order of things had been restored. I suppose it was the American flag and *Yankee Doodle Dandy* playing on the fifes, something that harkened back to my childhood, to the world of peace and prosperity I had known and would never know again.

But that sense of relief and nostalgia did not last. Life was hard under the occupation. The shelling stopped, but there was not enough food, and no one had any money. The servants became more and more irresponsible and unresponsive. Some left altogether, wandering off without even a word of goodbye, after they had spent their whole lives with us.

The news of Lee's surrender came within weeks. General Johnson fought on for a while afterwards, but we knew the Confederacy was finished. It ended when those colored soldiers marched up the street.

A few days later, the ships full of Negroes came steaming into the harbor. It was a celebration of their victory. We watched as if we were in a nightmare from which we couldn't awaken. I stood on East Battery as the *Planter* came in, the ship that had been stolen by that slave Small. It came steaming in from Fort Sumter, absolutely overflowing with people. It would be no exaggeration to say there were thousands of people on that ship. Mostly Negroes, but plenty of whites, too, carrying on the wildest celebration. We could hear cheering and singing a mile away as they approached the Southern Pier, where the ship had been stolen years before. Small himself was the captain. The drunken baboon crashed the ship into another steamer as he approached the dock, crushing the other boat's pilot house and sending the crowd scrambling to the far sides of each ship.

The ships rolled as the crowd fled, and I thought for a moment they would actually capsize. Small backed his ship away, with a crunching and tearing of wood, and the rowdy crowd cheered him. He stepped out of the wheelhouse and waved his hat, quite the dandy. He was surprisingly small and young, black as the ace of spades, but with most confident manner. He brought his ship in to the pier as the crowd cheered and a Yankee band played. The inmates had taken over the asylum. We were to live the next decade or so of our lives in a state ruled by these drunken, carousing darkies.

Some time later, I saw Small on the street, introducing a Yankee general to Captain Ferguson and Mr. Simmons, the men from whom Small had stolen the ship. Smalls talked with the white men as if he were a welcome guest in my own drawing room. He did have courteous manners, but it was as if one were watching a dog walk on its hind legs and speak. Most disconcerting, I remember.

Mrs. Towles asked if I would like to be introduced to Small. I think she had lost her mind.

The Good Neighbor

The secret to Robert Smalls is his Jewish blood. His father was a Jewish gold merchant from Charleston, a friend of John McKee's who was visiting the McKee home in Beaufort when he mounted a house servant one night and sired the future King of Beaufort County. I've known General Smalls most of my adult life, now. I first made his acquaintance when I returned to Beaufort after the war, and I think I am somewhat qualified to put forward this assessment.

I read this month a Mark Twain piece in Harper's magazine about the Jews. As I read, it occurred to me what had made Robert Smalls the way he is. He is half Jew, half darky, and the resulting mix is the most amazing and amusing of creatures.

First, let me quote Twain himself on a number of the Jew's characteristics:

> ... the Jew is a good and orderly citizen. Summed up, ... he is quiet, peaceable, industrious, unaddicted to high crimes and brutal dispositions; ... his family life is commendable; ... he is not a burden upon public charities; ... he is not a beggar; ... in benevolence he is above the reach of competition. These are the very quint-essentials of good citizenship. If you can add that he is as honest as the average of his neighbors - But I think that question is affirmatively answered by the fact that he is a successful business man.
>
> The basis of successful business is honesty; a business cannot thrive where the parties to it cannot trust each other. In the matter of numbers of the Jew counts for little in the overwhelming population of New York; but that his honesty counts for much is guaranteed by the fact that the immense wholesale business houses of Broadway, from the Battery to Union Square, is substantially in his hands. I suppose that the most picturesque example in history of a trader's trust in his fellow-trader was one where it was not Christian trusting Christian, but Christian trusting Jew.
>
> ...The Jew has his other side. He has some discreditable ways, though he has not a monopoly of them, because he cannot get entirely rid of vexatious Christian competition. We have seen that he seldom transgresses the laws against crimes of violence. Indeed, his dealings with courts are almost restricted to matters connected with commerce. He has a reputation for various small forms of cheating, and for practising oppressive usury, and for burning himself out to get the insurance, and for arranging cunning contracts which leave him an exit but lock the other man in, and for smart evasions which find him safe and comfortable just within the strict letter of the law, when court and jury know very well that he has violated the spirit of it.

And I add one further direct quote from Twain, which I think accounts for much of the story of Robert Smalls:

> ...the merits and demerits being fairly weighed and measured on both sides, the Christian can claim no superiority over the Jew in the matter of good citizenship. Yet in all countries, from the dawn of history, the Jew has been persistently and implacably hated, and with frequency persecuted.

When I came home from the war, I was thankful to find Beaufort spared the destruction I had seen in so many other cities on my journey home. The place was much changed. It was run-down and destitute, but at least it had not been blown up or burned by the Yankees.

I came home to find Robert Smalls was my next-door neighbor. The house in which he had lived as a young slave had come up for public auction in the last year of the war, and he had bought it, using some of the prize money the Yankees paid him for stealing the *Planter,* I hear. He was living there with his wife and children and his mother. The house was in better repair than most houses in Beaufort at that time (as it has been ever since). Smalls lived handsomely on his payroll as a Yankee ship captain.

The world had turned upside down, but I've never been one to shy away from a new reality. I met Smalls fairly soon after my return. He was courtly and gentlemanly in demeanor and most pleasant to me. Indeed, he has always been the most pleasant and agreeable of neighbors. We were young men when we first met. Our appearance has changed greatly in the decades since. As a young man, Smalls was short and slender. He was quite dark-skinned. It was difficult to see the white blood in him, but if you spent any time around him, you could quickly tell he was half-Jew, for no blue-gum darky ever talked or behaved or dealt as sharply as Bob Smalls.

Hannah, his first wife, was a diminutive woman. She was shy, a bit pinched in countenance, and apparently somewhat older than Smalls. I never liked her as much as I liked him, but she gave me no reason to complain as a neighbor.

Shortly after the war, Smalls's former owner, Mrs. McKee, appeared at their house. She had been widowed during the war and was older and diminished. She was destitute, as so many of us were. How she summoned the courage to ask Smalls, her former slave, for help, I'll never know. As the years went by, she suffered from hardening of the arteries, and for a while she entertained the delusion that she was mistress and owner of the home once more. But when she first moved in, she was entirely within her wits, and the humiliation must have been almost beyond bearing.

There was a rumor around town that her late husband, Henry McKee, was Smalls's father, and that Lydia (Smalls's mother) had been Henry's concubine. I knew Henry (and Lydia, for that matter) in the years before the war, and I have always considered that to be an unreasonable assertion. Lydia was twenty years older than Henry, and, as far as I could tell, he considered her his black mammy. However, tongues will wag, and Mrs. McKee can't have been ignorant of the rumors. Her humiliation in approaching Smalls for help must have been all the greater.

Smalls was gracious. He gave Mrs. McKee the master bedroom again (I often saw her brushing her hair by lantern light in the evenings up there,) while he crowded his large family in the rest of the place.

In many ways, Smalls was more Jew than darky. He was such an astute businessman that in the years immediately following the war, he became an extensive owner of property in the county. He owned plantations on Lady's Island, his store downtown, several other businesses, the large house on Prince Street, and many rental houses. In all my years living beside him in Beaufort, as much as I heard him excoriated or praised for his politics, I never heard anyone accuse him of dishonesty in business dealings. He was shrewd. He was tough. But he was, to the best of my knowledge, always fair and honest in business.

Smalls was also quite a proud man. I suppose we could attribute that to the Jew in him as well. I observed, recently, a biting example of that pride. Only four or five years ago, a young white man approached Smalls's house on some business. He found Smalls sitting in a rocking chair on the front porch. Smalls was, as we both had become by that time, a portly, older man. His hair was graying. The young white man addressed Smalls respectfully as "Uncle" and started to state his business.

Smalls bristled. He rose to his full height from his chair.

"If I were indeed your uncle, young man," he said, "then you would have to be my brother's child. However, I know for a fact that my only brother died many years ago and left no children behind. So that cannot be the case."

The younger man stood perplexed at the edge of the street for a long moment. Smalls stared down at him from the porch. And then the young man understood what Smalls wanted. He addressed my neighbor as "General," and the conversation carried forward civilly.

In my many years of living next door to this most uppity of niggers, I must confess, as much as the white race has vilified him elsewhere in South Carolina and throughout the nation, I find him to be an upright, kind, and honest man. I have never visited his house as a guest. This is, I suppose, as it should be. Yet we have spoken often, and we have never exchanged a cross word or had an unpleasant moment. And, although I would never admit to it in public, many is the time I have cast my secret ballot in an election for Smalls the politician.

The Brother

I rode with Brother Smalls in 1867 to attend what I believe was the first meeting of the Republican Party in South Carolina. It would not be inaccurate, I think, to call Robert Smalls the founder of the South Carolina Republican party, for no man at that meeting did more to see to its establishment and viability, and, certainly no man has ever done as much in loyal service to said party.

At that first meeting Brother Smalls was in an element to which he was clearly unaccustomed. You would never guess he would become the eloquent, fiery politician he was in future years. At that time, he was a sea captain, only recently returned from the war, and a man quite busy with his many business ventures throughout the sea islands. He was far from the most talkative man in the assembly, and, frankly, he was hampered by his own lack of education.

I have since learned he was taking determined strides at that very juncture to overcome this impediment. I understand a tutor visited his home for two hours every morning, teaching Brother Smalls how to read and write, and that Brother Smalls studiously read a newspaper every morning after the tutor left.

Politics is a dirty business, unfortunately, and in the years to come after the war, it would become far dirtier than any of us imagined. But I remember Brother Smalls when he rose to speak at that first meeting. He evoked the memory of the Great Emancipator himself. Smalls said that we, as receivers of the Emancipator's gift of grace, must do everything in our power to spread, cultivate, and maintain that gift in this world and amongst the future generations.

There are times when a man speaks the truth, and everyone listening knows it is the truth, and they just fall silent. Such was Brother Smalls's impact upon that meeting.

Uncle Romulus

A couple of years ago, *Sixty Minutes* reported on the controversial inclusion of *The Adventures of Huckleberry Finn* in American high school curricula. The controversy centers on that word- the "N-word," so profoundly obscene now that it must not be spoken in public, except on a hip-hop recording, or in a movie, or if the speaker is African-American, or... The word is upsetting to African-American students required to read it over and over through three or four hundred pages of what their teachers tell them is the greatest American novel.

Sixty Minutes interviewed a prestigious African-American professor of literature. Before he discussed *Huckleberry Finn* with a college class, he said, he had the class say the "N" word out loud, twenty times, just to get them over it.

I've tried that a couple of times with my college classes. I can't get them to say the word at all. I'll say it myself a few times out loud. They laugh nervously.

My students often discuss "nigger," because it shows up so often in the stories in their freshman English anthology. They are terrified of the word. It seems to be at least as profane to them, as, say, "motherfucker." But I don't remember ever seeing "motherfucker" in their literature anthology.

Shall I write, "motherfucker," twenty times for you?

The discussion pops up after my students read "A Rose for Emily" by Faulkner. A student will mention how offended they were by the extensive use of THAT word. THAT word is only used three times in "A Rose for Emily", if I remember correctly. They never notice that. I have to point it out to them.

Well, there is also that other offensive word, in the story, they say: "Negro."

Faulkner's use of the "N-word" (the worse of the two "N-words") is then inevitably proclaimed by some class member to be reflective of "the way people talked back in the day."

The students miss the point of the word in the story, I feel. The word was included, as it almost always is in American or British literature, to gouge into the reader's complacency.

In his 1927 story, Faulker uses "nigger" as the offensive word it was at the time he wrote, near the peak of the ethnic cleansing in Mississippi and South Carolina. By the ethnic cleansing, I mean what is commonly referred to as the Jim Crow era- but more on that later.

Marshall Evans

Twain published *The Adventures of Huckleberry Finn* in 1884, the last year Robert Smalls was elected to Congress. Smalls was, in that session, one of only two African-American members remaining in Congress. Twain was writing a book about American culture and about American hatred of the African part of ourselves, that hatred so central to our national being. I think Twain meant every single use of the word "nigger" in that book to be a slap right in the face of the reader. It may be the way people talked back then, but it was as offensive then as it is today. It was a word many, many people used, but only people like Huckleberry Finn, the hapless child of the town drunk, might use it to describe all black people, including his closest friend, in all situations all the time. Twain would expect his audience to recoil.

This begs the question: why is "nigger" such an offensive word? "Motherfucker," that's offensive. None of us wants to be accused of fucking our own mother, for goodness' sake!

"Motherfucker," "sonofabitch," "whore," "bastard," these words can be insults in that they describe something none of us would particularly like to be.

But "nigger" describes what? Being black? Being of African descent? How does that get to be an insult?

Why do my students think "Negro" is offensive? Is it the same etymological progression that makes "colored" offensive, or that appears, in some circles, to be making "black" move in the same direction?

128

Why have these words- over the years cultivated as the "polite" way to denote African ancestry- now become nearly as offensive as that most dreaded word?

Is it because those words, too, describe the thing no one wants to be?

I suspect the "N-word" has become a great public taboo in the early 21st Century because it exposes that American self-hatred. We all know how we really feel. We just would rather pretend we didn't feel that way.

We can allow people who are obviously descended from Africans to use the "N-word" because we like it. It hurts so good. It hurts the way the troubled teenager feels when she cuts herself or gets a tattoo.

When my niece Grace was in the mental hospital, a couple of months before she died, her doctors said her cutting and tattoos betrayed a secret self-hatred, a tendency toward self-destruction she needed to be aware of. She was in great danger of taking her own life, they told her. She discussed this with me in the longest, closest discussion we ever had. Our discussion was so close and so intense that one of the hospital attendants walked over, ostensibly to adjust the visiting room curtains right behind Grace. I realized the attendant was really listening to see if our conversation was dangerous. Was I one of the abusers?

We talked about Grace's childhood- the serial, abusive step-fathers, her mother's illness. Her mother's suicide. My own near-suicide and hospitalization. It was a long conversation about secrets we never wanted to face. It was a look into the abyss, into the darkness that threatened to overwhelm us.

I'm really digressing.

One last thought on the "N-word." In an earlier episode, when my friend Jacob and I were in the now-vanished Robert Smalls exhibit at the Tabernacle Baptist Church, I recounted a story where Smalls beat a white man with his cane in front of a liquor store in Beaufort. My version of that story does not entirely coincide with the historical record as I have found it.

The white man did emerge from the liquor store, where, according to historical accounts, he encountered Smalls on the sidewalk. The white man said something derogatory to Smalls, prompting the very public and very thorough beating. But historical accounts do not specify the nature of the derogatory comment.

I, in my telling of the story to Jacob, said the white man had called Smalls a "nigger." It seemed to me this was the most likely insult to provoke a public beating from a prominent U.S. Congressman.

On further reflection, I wonder if that was truly the insult. If that is what the man called him, would Smalls have reacted the way he did? Surely, all his life, "nigger" had simply been what he was. It would, perhaps, be like calling me "baldy," or "double-chin." Would "nigger" have provoked rage?

No, I now think the insult may have been something else entirely. Did he call Smalls a thief? The incident took place after Smalls's trial and conviction, I think. And a thief would have been a thing Smalls really didn't want to be.

Uncle Romulus

I know. It's a novel. You're not supposed to look at tables of data. But please study the following carefully:

Population Mix in South Carolina by Census Year

Source: U.S. Census Bureau

Census	Percent White	Percent Black
1860	41	59
1870	41	59
1890	40	60
1930	54	46
1960	65	35

What happened to all the black people? Where did they go? Were the whites really that much more prolific at breeding?

Now, please read the following from the Convention on the Prevention and Punishment of the Crime of Genocide, adopted by the United Nations General Assembly on the ninth of December, 1948, as Resolution 260 (III) A:

Definition of Genocide:

Article II: In the present Convention, genocide means ANY of the following acts committed with intent to destroy, in whole or in part, a national, ethnical, racial or religious group, as such:

(a) Killing members of the group;
(b) Causing serious bodily or mental harm to members of the group;
(c) Deliberately inflicting on the group conditions of life calculated to bring about its physical destruction in whole or in part;

And look at this information from the United Nations Office of the Special Advisor on the Prevention of Genocide:

The following factors cumulatively increase the risk of genocide:

- *Tense inter-group relations, including a record of discrimination and/or other human rights violations committed against a group;*
- *Weak institutional capacity to prevent genocide, such as the lack of an independent judiciary, ineffective national human rights institutions, the absence of international actors capable of protecting vulnerable groups, and a lack of impartial security forces and media;*
- *The presence of illegal arms and armed elements;*
- *Underlying political, economic, military or other*

motivation to target a group;

- *Circumstances that facilitate perpetration of genocide, such as a sudden or gradual strengthening of the military or security apparatus;*
- *Acts that could be elements of genocide, such as killings, abduction and disappearances, torture, rape and sexual violence, "ethnic cleansing" or pogroms or the deliberate deprivation of food;*
- *Evidence of the "intent to destroy in whole or in part";*
- *Triggering factors, such as elections.*

And, finally, please review this definition of "ethnic cleansing" in United Nations Security Council Resolution 780, passed on the sixth of October, 1992:

Ethnic cleansing is a purposeful policy designed by one ethnic or religious group to remove by violent and terror-inspiring means the civilian population of another ethnic or religious group from certain geographic areas.

I will leave you to ponder these exhibits, and we will return to the subject later.

The Citizen

In etteen hunned and sitty et, they let colored vote. I go line up on election day and talk to eboddy and make up my own mind and vote. Like a human bean.

The whites was so damn mad they let the colored vote aint hardly none of em come out and vote theyseff. Which who care, is how I feel. They mo of us an they is of them anyway, so how they goin outvote us?

Anyway, we lect Robert Smalls to go to the convention, and he tell me they mos of the people at that convention is colored. It like a black pahdise, he say, how the Laud done set thing aright at last. Most the folk in the stet be colored, and they finally got colored makin the law.

And Smalls he say they goin have school for all the chillun, colored and po white too, that it in the Constitution now. Which, how people goin send they chap to school when they need em work in the field with em? But that Robert, he aint think like you and me.

I aint hardly blame him for it, and I reckon that why I love him so, he a good man, that true. But you got yo dream world what they preach bout in chuch, and you got yo real world. You know zactly what I mean. And aint nobody evuh really live in that dream world. We all gots to live in the real world, all I sayin.

That all I got to say. I love the man. I really do. He a fine man, only you go up to Columbia in yo fine carriage and yo fine suit of clothes and making constitution and what not, and you ain really nothing but a colored boy no matter how much you dream.

A Fellow Citizen

The absurdity of the current situation evades imagination. A convention is gathered in Columbia to write a new constitution, so that we, at the point of a bayonet, may submit to rejoin the Union. Virtually no whites- none of my personal acquaintance- have voted for delegates to this sham gathering. I understand the majority of the delegates are ignorant darkies, field hands and barbers and blacksmiths, gathered now in fine suits of clothes to rewrite our state constitution.

No good will come of it. No good could possibly come of it. The able statesmen and politicians of our noble state are simply biding their time, awaiting the hour when reason will prevail and law and order are once again restored.

The new constitution, I hear, gives near universal suffrage to the Negro, placing our government in the hands of illiterate former slaves, who by their sheer numbers will drive us toward chaos and oblivion. Universal, free education is promised. As if these nincompoops could be taught anything. They plan to take the spawn of the ignorant bluegum, send him to a school, and convert him into something other than the field hand he was born to be?

It is a colossal waste of time and taxpayer money. The only viable education for the people of Charleston will continue to be private schooling paid for by the ruling class themselves. These public schools, if they ever come into being at all, will simply be warehouses for an unruly brood of shiftless Negroes and white trash.

The Scalawag

I member the first time a man called me a scalawag to my face. I stepped in Broward's Saloon in Columbia, one afternoon after a session of the legislature done adjourned, and they was a white, fat lawyer in his suit standing at the corner of the bar, and he said out loud, to everybody around him, "Well, and here come the scalawags."

Maybe I should a called him outside. But I reckon at the time, I was feeling kind of better than him, me being an elected member of the legislature, and I just carried myself like I was above it.

Which, truth be told, I was. I don't care that terribly much about it now. It's been thirty some odd years since I was a member of the Republican party. I seen the tide a shiftin, and if a man caint go where the wind blows, then he oughtn't be out in the wind. That's where a politician is all the time, out in the wind, a tryin to make his way like a sailor on the sea. You go where the wind will take you.

Course, at that time, the wind was blowin out of the north, and ifn a man was to run for public office in South Carolina, which I'd always had a hankering to do, then he might as well count on joinin up with the Republicans.

To hear people talk nowadays, it was nothing but a bunch of thievin niggers and drunk, carpetbaggin yankees that took over the government and run it like it was their private till. But they's a lot of exaggeration in that. They was some decent, God-fearin men tried to do right, and they was some thievin rascals. It pretty much was the way it is now, and from what I can tell, the way it always been in South Carolina politics.

Now, one thing that was missing from that government in the years after the war, was General Hampton and his high-born sort. There was plenty of high-born Yankees with a right smart of education, more education, truth be told, than Wade Hampton and any of his kind. But the Southern planters and the old money, they was pretty much left out of the government by the Constitution of 1868, because, truth be told, that Constitution basically let all free men vote. Which, if you look around you at all, would put the rich at a pretty damn harsh disadvantage in this state. They ain't enough of em put together to elect a dog catcher.

Now, the fact of the matter was, and it still is, that the majority of the population of South Carolina is niggers. And if them niggers is free men, and citizens of the United States of America, which the Constitution of the United States says they is, like it or not, it wouldn't be any great surprise to find that most of the Representatives in the House would turn out to be colored after a free and clear election.

Now, having wandered a bit off the subject, let me get back to this man Robert Smalls, who I got to know when I was in the legislature.

When I first met Robert Smalls, he weren't that much different than any of them other niggers in the statehouse, except he was a good bit blacker than most, a right smart of them bein so high yellow you'd easily mistake em for bein a white man. But Smalls was a kind of plump, kinky-haired darky. He dressed like a dandy, and he drove a fancy barouche. He carried a walking cane with a gold handle, and he cut a figure, I've got to admit.

He was a quiet man. You knew he'd been in the war and seen real action. He tended not to speak too much in those first couple of sessions of the legislature.

But all them other niggers knew of him, how he had stolen a ship right out of Charleston Harbor in the war and delivered it to the Yankee fleet. They all perked up and listened when he did have something to say.

I liked Smalls. I liked him a lot. I found he was a clear thinker and an honest man.

Now, you may wonder how I'm talking about a nigger this way. Well, it really was different back then, is all I can say. The rich was poor and the poor was rich, and the highfalutin was desperate and the redneck might be king. And in that time, a nigger might dress and act just as much like a fine gentleman as anybody else.

Back then, in the days after the war, the ones like Robert Smalls come out and run things just like Wade Hampton and Pitchfork Ben Tillman did later on. Some of them, not Smalls, mind you, but some of the other high-yellow ones, was as educated as any New York lawyer, and they'd stand up in the legislature and carry on like they was Daniel Webster, I'll tell you.

Course at the same time, they was a passel of just plain old coons in there, too.

It was strange times. I went down there meaning to do my best, and to help folks. I figgered we had to rebuild after the war, and somebody had best step up and make things better for everybody else. I'd say the most of the people in that legislature, or a damn good many of them, was there because they wanted to make things better, to build up the state, you know, from the mess we was in at the time.

Smalls sponsored the bill to provide free public schoolin for every child in the state- white, black, poor, redneck. You know, they was a time when most folks didn't have any kind of schoolin at all.

Now, as to how a old scalawag like me got to be a respected Democratic member of the Legislature these forty odd years later, well, politics is a fine art, I tell you, and some of us is born with the talent and some ain't. That's a fact, I reckon. They ain't many folks in Greenville County would tell in public that I was one of the original scalawags in the South Carolina legislature. Everybody done found it more convenient, I reckon, to forget that part, sort of like they done forgot them eloquent, educated, high-yellow niggers in the Legislature.

You cain't tell nobody that these days, and Lord knows, I ain't about to start trying. People hear what they want to hear, and believe what they want to believe, and they make up the stories they need to make em believe it. I ain't lying to you. I'm just telling it like it is.

The Public Record

Whereas, thirty states of the American Union have ratified the fifteenth Amendment to the Constitution of the United State; and whereas, this action of the American people fixes our government firmly on the side of right, and makes it a beacon of light to the nations of the earth, and our flag the emblem of liberty, and the aegis of every citizen beneath its fold throughout the length and breadth of our land and the world over, and whereas, it is eminently proper that this great event should be hailed with joy and thanksgiving; therefore:

Be it resolved... that, as an expression of our deep sense of gratitude to the Almighty God for this victory of right, and in honor of this event, His Excellency, the Governor, be requested to set apart a day of Thanksgiving and prayer immediately after the official notice of the ratification has been promulgated.

- Resolution introduced by Representative Robert Smalls in the South Carolina House of

Representatives, February, 1870. This resolution passed both houses of the legislature and was ratified by the Governor.

Section 1. The right of citizens of the United States to vote shall not be denied or abridged by the United States or by any State on account of race, color, or previous condition of servitude.

Section 2. The Congress shall have power to enforce this article by appropriate legislation.

– *Fifteenth Amendment to the United States Constitution*

The Great, Great

I served as an officer in the 13th South Carolina Infantry. I rarely mention it. My family and friends speak of it often as a point of pride. But the memories are too dark for me.

I can list the major battles we fought in: Second Manassas, Fredricksburg, Chancellorsville, Gettysburg, The Wilderness, Spotsylvania, Petersburg (we were in the Breakthrough), and Appomattox Court House. I was paroled at Appomattox with General Lee- and with less than a third of the men who had mustered in with us at Columbia the first year of the war.

By the end, by the Breakout at Petersburg, I was a man moving through a nightmare. The bullets tearing through the men around me, the shells blowing them to pieces- it became a weird kind of normal to me at the end. The Breakout at Petersburg was the worst.

I don't see how I wasn't killed. Men were killed like mowing wheat down in a field with a scythe. What was the point?

But that is the past, and I'm thinking now of the danger our country finds itself in.

Colored folk can't run the world, any more than the women and children of the world could take over and run all the families. That's why I got involved with the Red Shirts. General Hampton was a respectable leader during the war. When he was called on to get the state of South Carolina back under control he stepped up to his duty, as I saw it, and I felt I had to step up to my duty, also.

We've got to be firm with these darkies, or they're not going to get the message. They were ruled for most of their lives with the lash, and they aren't going to understand the facts until they've had some rough treatment. I'm not afraid of being rough when it's necessary.

Uncle Romulus

My father informs me his great grandfather served in the 13th South Carolina infantry. I've known of this great grandfather all my life. His folding desk stands in my living room. A framed map entitled "The Seat of War in South Carolina" hangs in our hallway, marked by his sweat stains. He carried it in the breast pocket of his uniform. His name and rank- Lieutenant- are written in cursive on the cover. These items were in my grandmother's house when I was a child. She spoke of them often and explained their significance to me.

She used to have his powder horn hanging by her fireplace. It wasn't really a horn. It was a metal bottle with a brass spout on one end. There was a trigger on the spout that discharged the correct amount of powder for the rifle. My grandmother showed me how it worked, and I was fascinated by it as a boy. I last saw it in my father's attic.

I never heard any details of this ancestor's actual service during the war, at least until my father let me know he had served in the 13th South Carolina Infantry. I looked up the regiment on the Internet, and there he was, right on the roster. And there was the list of engagements they had fought. My great, great grandfather had been on the front lines of nearly every major battle of the war in Virginia, Maryland, and Pennsylvania, all the way up to the surrender at Appomattox.

He must not have spoken about those battles to his family, though. The lore was never passed down.

My grandmother was a genealogist. She was quite accomplished at it. She published a book in the 1950's tracing her family throughout its history in South Carolina, going back to the original land grant in what is now Richfield County in the mid-1700's.

She also did extensive research on what she called "Allied Families," tracing many spouses' families as far as she could find records. One of those families was her husband's- my grandfather's.

But her ability to trace that family was hampered by a missing link in the early 1800's. She could trace his family line as far as Charleston in the early 1800's, and she could pick up the family again in South Carolina, living along the Pee Dee River, well back into the 1700's. Family lore connected the folks in Charleston with the earlier relatives on the Pee Dee. But my grandmother could never find a direct link in the records between the two groups. There was one generation missing.

Years after she passed away, my father became interested in genealogy himself. Empowered by the Internet, he could accomplish much more than my grandmother.

And he dug into the mystery of the missing link in his father's family.

After Grace died, Dad first explained to me the mystery of the missing link. He was convinced he could, with his modern Internet tools, find the answer to the puzzle.

"You need to get your head into this," he said. "You're good at thinking these things through. You're better at it than I am."

He gave me everything he had on the subject.

He had photocopies of the church records near the Pee Dee, where the family had been before the missing link.

There were delightful accounts of church brethren excommunicated for drinking, fornication, or adultery, and sometimes reinstated after getting right with God. And there was a fascinating, and unexpected, relationship between the African and the European parishioners. There was little social distance between them. The Africans were, I supposed, the slaves of the Europeans at the time. (Realistically, they could have also been free people- a situation that was not rare.) At any rate the blacks and the whites occupied rather similar places in the church registry. They were born, died, married, confessed their faith in the Lord, were baptized, fell into sin, were punished, were sometimes forgiven, and were brought back into the fold. They were not markedly different. They apparently attended the same services in the same small church and were enrolled by hand in the same record book.

My solution to the genealogical mystery began to occur to me as I read this church record.

Uncle Romulus

Several years ago, when I was working in the South Carolina Governor's Office as a speech writer, the Chief of Staff and I were researching a response to some legislative skulduggery. I was in the Chief of Staff's office, thumbing through his law books, consulting the South Carolina Constitution of 1895, written in a convention attended by Robert Smalls.

As I was leafing through the Constitution, sitting in the visitor's chair beside the Chief of Staff's desk, I ran across a shocking entry, a clause specifically banning the marriage of whites and blacks in the state of South Carolina.

"My God, Horace," I said. "Have you ever seen this?" Horace, the chief of staff, was a learned attorney, a very dark-skinned Geechee of my generation. He had grown up in Frogmore, a tiny village in Beaufort County. Horace, a Harvard law graduate, was the most upright and proper of men and a staunchly conservative Republican.

Horace glanced at the miscegenation clause.

"Oh yeh," he chuckled. "I'm pretty sure they repealed that already."

That incident, and his less-than-satisfactory dismissal, led me to research the matter on my own time.

The miscegenation clause of the 1895 constitution had, as Horace stated, been repealed. In 1967, the U.S. Supreme Court declared all such state laws (there were many across the nation) unconstitutional.

The South Carolina Legislature eventually got around to acting on the Supreme Court's decision, but they were in no hurry. In the 1999-2000 Legislative session, the legislature repealed the miscegenation ban- *thirty-two years* after the Supreme Court declared it unconstitutional.

In case you're wondering why it took them so long, consider this: In 1998, the legislature had put the question on the ballot for South Carolina voters to decide. But 38% of voters in the state voted to keep the clause, an insufficient margin to amend the constitution. The legislature was forced to take their own courageous stand as the new millennium broke.

The real push to ban marriage between blacks and whites had come after the Civil War, when Robert Smalls was involved in politics. In this era, the "one-drop" doctrine evolved, meaning that anyone who had one drop of African blood was to be considered a Negro under the law.

This one-drop rule of racial identity became the norm throughout the United States. It is so ingrained in our culture today that virtually none of us is aware of our own reliance on the standard. We instantly and easily identify our fellow citizens as "black" or "white," and this doesn't seem strange to us at all.

Witness the near-complete death of the term "mulatto" in our culture.

When I first proposed miscegenation to my father as a solution to his genealogical quandary, he was irritated and dismissive. We were white people. My proposal made no sense. Black people can have European ancestry, of course. But white people can't.

I continued to jokingly propose the "nigger in the woodpile" theory to Dad over the following year, just to watch his reaction. Then, one day, a couple of weeks after I told Dad about the book I was writing on Robert Smalls, he spoke about the African-American ancestor in our line (his great, great, great grandfather) as if that black man were a fact, as if the story were now true.

We were discussing the historical controversy surrounding Robert Smalls's parentage, and Dad said, "Well, it's like that black man you say is in our family tree. They wouldn't have discussed it back then. They never would have talked about it all. Nobody. That's just the way it was. That's the way Southern culture was. I know. I lived through it."

And that became our story.

I never told Dad about the DNA test showing I have 4.3% African ancestry. That may not seem like much, at first glance, but if the ancestor he was talking about was a full-blooded African, that would only amount to 1.6% African ancestry. So there had to be others. How did they get in there?

I probably won't tell him all that.

This story of mixed ancestry in our family is far from unique. There are, of course, many, many Americans of mixed European and African ancestry.

For instance, Robert Smalls's daughter married Samuel Bampfield from Charleston after the Civil War. Samuel Bampfield's father was an Englishman, and his mother was a free African-American. Samuel's parents lived together as a married couple in pre-Civil War Charleston- openly. They appear to have had some considerable social standing.

The English heritage in the Bampfield line can still clearly be seen in photographs of Smalls's descendants today. The Bampfield-Smalls union yielded some dozen children. These descendants later spread across the United States, fleeing the ethnic cleansing campaign in the South for refugee status in the North. There they led successful lives in the segregated demimonde of 20th-Century Black America, as educators and professionals, attending Negro colleges and universities. The descendants in this line, at least as far as one can tell from published family photographs, are quite light-skinned.

Which makes one part of the Robert Smalls story a bit more mysterious to me. Why did General Smalls himself propose and champion the anti-miscegenation clause of the 1895 constitution? That may surprise you. It surprised me. But it's historical fact. It is part of the story of his participation in that convention. Here is the clause, formerly residing in Article III, Section 33:

> *"The marriage of a white person with a Negro or mulatto, or person who shall have 1/8 or more of Negro blood, shall be unlawful and void."*

At the same constitutional convention, Smalls also proposed that the illegitimate children of white fathers and Negro mothers be given legal status as heirs of the white fathers.

The mostly white convention delegates roundly laughed that particular proposal out of consideration.

The Truth Seeker

After a career in journalism, I welcome the opportunity just to tell the truth. The plain, unvarnished truth.

You see, as a journalist, your living depends entirely on your ability to sell newspapers. People buy newspapers because the papers tell them stories they want to hear. When a man opens up a newspaper in the morning or in the evening, he is sitting down secure in the fantasy that he understands the world as it is, that his understanding is complete and right, and that only those fools who disagree with him stand between him and the possibility of establishing a true paradise on earth.

You cannot make a living telling people what they don't want to hear or presenting evidence that their world view might in some way be incomplete.

So a journalist, or anyone who makes a living telling stories, for that matter, has to know up front what his boundaries are, and he has to tailor his story to fit within those boundaries imposed by his audience. Thus, his ability to tell the truth is enormously circumscribed.

I would like, then, to attempt to tell the truth about Robert Smalls. I would like to tell it here, before Almighty God, and no one else, since I think that truth has never really been told.

You see, Robert Smalls was never allowed to be a man. He was never allowed to be a child of God, a point in the universe around which the Almighty constructed one of his magnificent realities. Instead, Smalls always has been, and, I fear, always will be someone else's story. His life has been twisted to fit the needs of whatever set of storytellers happens to be ascendant in the moment. The Yankee, the Red Shirt, the Negro, the Abolitionist, the Civil Rights advocate, the White Supremacist, the Democrat, the Republican, the believer-- all these people have a need to tell Smalls's story in the way they want it told, and none of them has ever just let him be who he was. I am as guilty as any other man.

But enough of my lecture. Let me begin my story.

I first encountered Smalls when he was a South Carolina state Senator. I was new to journalism. My uncle had offered me a job writing copy for his paper. He had provided the majority of my support since my father died in the war, so I had no thought of doing anything else.

By the time I met Smalls, he was quite the successful politician, by reputation one of the few honest men in the state Senate. People knew Smalls was an upright man in a town where graft was a way of life.

I think what made this more outrageous to his enemies was that he was the leader of one of the most dynamic and well-oiled political machines in the state. He was becoming the King of Beaufort County. Beaufort County was fairly prosperous in the years after the war. And the county had a four-fifths Negro majority.

Smalls had made himself rich, using his Yankee payroll from the war years to finance a number of businesses and investments. The Negroes in Beaufort looked up to him as a war hero, a savior, a god of sorts. He was a Major General in the militia, which gave him the opportunity to dress in a flashy uniform and arm a phalanx of similarly-dressed Negroes to march behind him in frequent parades. He was also the founder of a marching brass band, which he produced for public performances on any convenient occasion.

I witnessed his band play several times at political rallies. They were delightful, playing the most raucous Negro music in the liveliest fashion. The crowd would start clapping, swaying and dancing, transported by the rhythm. Smalls bounced as he led the band, smiling and lording over his exultant subjects as if he were their true deliverer.

Smalls could work his magic on the Negro voters of Beaufort County, and if there is one thing politicians envy more than anything else, it is this ability to work a voodoo spell on the electorate. It is the thing politicians live for, the air they breathe.

This was the Robert Smalls I first met, a portly, middle-aged state Senator, a very dark-skinned Negro, the most delightful and charming of men, eloquent and persuasive, unusually quick-witted in a profession not populated by many quick-witted men. He was a war hero, but he was a hero to the Enemy. This made him a demon to the whites of South Carolina.

Not long after I met him, he was elected to the United States Congress. A short time later, General George Armstrong Custer led a U.S. Army regiment into a slaughter on the Little Big Horn River in Wyoming Territory, and trouble began.

American public opinion, it has been my observation over the years, cannot stay fixed on any one goal for very long. A decade is a long, long time for the American electorate to stand behind an idea. By the time of the Centennial, American enthusiasm for reforming the former states of the Confederacy was waning.

Chief Sitting Bull led the most effective military action in the history of America's Indian wars, and instantly, the American public found another thing to focus on. The Army was needed to protect decent, white people from rampaging Indians out west. It certainly couldn't be expected to sit around in the former Confederacy, protecting a bunch of darkies from their neighbors.

Within a couple of weeks of the Little Big Horn, Ben Tillman saw his opening.

Tillman, as formidable as he was in later years- champion of the common man, savior of the Western farmer, famous Pitchfork Ben Tillman- was nothing but a one-eyed redneck when I first saw him.

He had lost the eye in an accident before the war, and he hadn't been able to serve because of it. For a white man of his generation to sit out the war was a soul-destroying sort of shame. That kind of thing can haunt a man his whole life- twist his personality for decades.

Tillman's opportunity came in Hamburg, a few days after the Centennial Celebration of the Declaration of Independence, a big affair among the Negroes, but one almost entirely boycotted by the white populace. As I understand what happened at Hamburg (and it is not easy to understand what really happened), a Negro militia was drilling on the public street when a white planter demanded to pass through in his carriage.

The commander of the Negro militia refused to take this order from a passing fellow citizen, a mere civilian. The militia, after all, were dressed in their fancy uniforms.

I suppose we all know how the man in the carriage felt. It all began simply enough. One man overplaying his hand as an agent of the government. Another man taking umbrage at that.

The man in the carriage was eventually allowed to pass. You might think things had been settled.

But Pitchfork Ben (a nickname given to him later in his career, when he said he would like to stick a pitchfork in the rear of President Cleveland) was the ablest of politicians, and he saw the moment to spring.

Tillman, on hearing of the confrontation, roused up a rabble of Red Shirt militia and recruited a Confederate General to lead them into action against the Negroes. Within a day, the Red Shirts had moved into Hamburg, cornered the Negro militiamen in the town hall, and reestablished the rule of the white man in that corner of Edgefield county.

After they were besieged the town hall for a while, the Negroes surrendered. The incident, once again, presented an opportunity for a peaceful and reasonable settlement. But Tillman didn't want peace, and he didn't want reason. I covered that man my entire career, and he wanted two things more than anything else. He wanted to be famous. And he wanted things done his way.

After the Negro militiamen in Hamburg surrendered, the Red Shirts summarily shot half a dozen of them in their backs as they tried to get away. This action established what I would call the "Tillman Doctrine", which was basically, a Negro's life is worth something less than a dog's.

By that time, Robert Smalls was a U.S. Congressman. Congress, reacting to the public outrage across the United States roused by the massacre- the massacre at Little Big Horn, where blond-haired white men had been murdered- was debating legislation to pull U. S. Army units out of the South and send them to the West to fight the Indians.

Smalls rose to speak against the move, pleading the Army units were the only thing standing between Southern blacks and widespread slaughter. He gave a detailed account of the Hamburg Massacre on the floor of the U. S. House of Representatives to prove his point. Northern papers picked up his speech. Smalls read a letter on the floor of the House from a South Carolinian who claimed to be an eye-witness to the event. This letter got to be the story, at least as it was reported in Northern papers. I rely largely on that story as I tell you of the incident these many years later. Perhaps I believe Northern papers more than I should. I should, after all, know better.

The letter Smalls was reading was anonymous. A fellow Congressman (a Democrat) challenged him several times in the debate to supply the name of the author.

"I will say to the gentleman," Smalls replied at last to one of these challengers, "if he is desirous that the name shall be given in order to have another Negro killed, he will not get it from me." This, it was reported in one Northern newspaper, was greeted with great applause on the floor of the House.

I, for my part, suspect the incidents at Hamburg took place much as Smalls described them. Reading the name of the letter's author there on the House floor (if that author had, in fact, been a Negro other than the Congressman himself) could conceivably have resulted in the death of said Negro.

However, I wonder whether the Democratic congressman who requested the name of the letter's author really had that result in mind at the time he requested the information. Maybe- maybe he was just looking for the truth.

The Great, Great

Ben Tillman was the one that got me involved in the trouble down in Hamburg. That one-eyed rascal. He probably wouldn't even raise his hat to me if we passed on the street now, but we were tight friends when he needed a mob to lynch some niggers.

He came riding up to the house itching for a fight. He was fired up, and he knew how to get others fired up. He did know that. He still knows that, I reckon.

Now, I am not one easily stirred. As I said before, four years at war in the 13th South Carolina was more than enough fighting for any ten men. But Ben had a point. This whole thing with the niggers had gone far enough. A man's got to know his place in the world. The world can't function if folks don't know their place. It's how everybody knows how to get along with each other.

Now, you say, I'm as much as a quarter colored myself. I know it. But folks in Newberry, as far as I can tell, only speak of it in hushed tones in the privacy of their homes. I suspect Ben Tillman has no more idea that I'm the grandson of a shine than fly to the moon.

Everybody knew these coloreds was getting out of hand. You saw them parading down the street in their militia uniforms, Yankee uniforms like they were some kind of soldier in the war, when the most any of them ever did was pick cotton and milk cows and cower in the bushes. You saw the ones that got a little money lording it around in their carriages and fine clothes like they were plantation owners.

So I put on a red shirt and grabbed my rifle and mounted my horse and rode down to Hamburg with Ben Tillman and his bunch.

General Butler, lately of the Confederate army, was placed in charge of the movement, and I felt comfortable following him. He'd shown himself to be a capable leader, a man who could be in charge.

I followed orders. We surrounded the barracks where the Negro militia was holed up. We held them at bay while talks went on, demanding they disarm and disband and stop terrorizing the local citizenry.

After a few hours' siege, they gave in and came out. General Butler ordered a trial of the worst of the rabble rousers, right there on the spot. Tillman played a large role in the trial, making the case for all the grievances the honest white people of that country had against this bunch.

I didn't realize what was going to come of it. I guess I should have. They strung four of them boys right up after the jury found them guilty. I didn't like it. I think proper channels should have been followed before they hung those boys.

I heard, although I didn't witness it, that they later dragged the colored policeman out of his house and shot him for his part in the whole affair.

They were rough on those niggers. They were. But they got their attention.

Uncle Romulus

None of us wanted to admit how troubled Grace was. Even after several diagnoses of mental illness, we wanted to pretend she was, by birth, just like the other kids in the family. We wanted to pretend her behavioral problems were due to her environment, that her mother had simply brought too much chaos into her life.

Nature or nurture. That is the question.

Let's consider, in comparison, Robert Smalls's childhood. We will probably never know who the boy's biological father was. There are many candidates, many theories, but almost no proof to establish the truth.

One biographer says while we don't know who Robert's biological father was, his sociological father was clearly Henry McKee. McKee kept his child slave Robert with him as a favorite-riding, hunting, touring his plantations. Young Robert lived a few steps behind the McKee house in a slave cabin with his mother. The environment appears to have been stable and loving. This description of Smalls's Beaufort childhood is consistent through all historical accounts. The idyllic nurturing is usually postulated to be the reason for Smalls's atypical trajectory later in life.

But, if Smalls was raised as a slave in Beaufort, South Carolina in the years before the Civil War, just how benign and fertile would his childhood really have been? Historical sources tell of his mother taking a very young Robert to see a slave whipped at the Beaufort Armory, ostensibly so Robert would understand the tenuousness of his status as a house slave and Mr. Henry's pet. Now, maybe you need to take a short stroll through the streets of modern Beaufort to put this story into perspective. The scene of this slave whipping (and, one assumes, many subsequent whippings and incarcerations and hangings of slaves) is only a couple of blocks from the idyllic McKee home.

Try to put yourself in the mind of a five- or six-year-old. Try to imagine the horror of watching a grown man, black like you, bound and whipped mercilessly by white men, men who looked very much like the kindly gentleman who kept you as his pet. Imagine this scene being repeated regularly, two or three blocks from your home, throughout your childhood.

On the other hand, let's look at the tradition passed down by Smalls's descendants. They maintain that Henry McKee, Smalls's owner, was his actual, biological father.

If Henry was the father, then this is the environment in which Smalls grew up: He lived as a slave in a small shanty behind the big house. He was the high-yellow love-child of his master. Robert's mother would have been that master's nanny- a slave who had raised Henry McKee- who had quite possibly been his wet nurse- and who was some twenty years Henry's senior. In this scenario, grown-up Henry had bedded his mammy and fathered a child, and now that child was his favorite.

McKee lived with his white wife in the big house a few steps away, with all his legitimate, white children, while Lydia, McKee's nanny/lover/baby-mama, cooked, cleaned and cared for McKee's white children (and his white wife) and Henry sported about the countryside with her child, his young, high-yellow pet.

And let's not forget, Henry's white widow later came (of her own volition) to live after the war in that same house with General Smalls, along with Lydia and a house full of Smalls's black relatives.

Well, my niece's dealings with her many step-live-ins, whether or not some of them were physically abusive or had substance problems or did far worse things, can hardly match the whackiness of the domestic scene I have described above. And the scenario I described above needs little conjecture. It is entirely consistent with historical fact and Smalls's own family tradition.

So, can we really say that Smalls's unnatural courage, *joie-de-vivre*, ability to transcend his environment, ability to inspire all around him to live on a higher plain of existence, ability to ignite vast conspiracies dedicated to his destruction, that all this was due to the environment in which he was raised?

Or was it due to nature? In which case, should we accept the argument that his father must have been possessed of some high-caliber, supercharged genetic material, the Ashkenazi Jew, perhaps? Smalls might have been (as he was rumored to be) one of that other, ancient race of feared, envied, hated, victims of genocide.

Or would he, alternatively, have borne the genes of the black field slave, an unheralded, unrecorded man by the name of Smalls, whose progenitors survived the brutal, alligator-infested, super-heated hell-fens that were Beaufort's rice plantations? Natural selection would have ensured that the Negro father, coming from a string of survivors in such other-worldly conditions, could spawn the most magnificent of human beings. The future General, a product of the evanescent, timeless hunt for love amid the slave cabins, then emerges as a superhuman blessed with the grace of God and the ability to survive in an unsurvivable universe.

Whatever. Smalls turned out to be what he was.

Grace turned out to be what she was.

Whatever.

The Great, Great

Robert Smalls stood up in the U.S. Congress and told his version of what happened in Hamburg, and let me tell you, it made people in South Carolina hopping mad. There are things you talk about, and things you don't.

The next time I was called out with the Red Shirts was when that carpetbagging Governor Chamberlain came to Edgefield to campaign. He had Congressman Smalls in tow. There was a huge crowd of coloreds turned out to meet them. I'm talking about maybe a couple of thousand of them gathered around the train station, waiting for their heroes to talk to them.

We had several hundred armed, white men in red shirts there to take control. And face it, any one white man with a gun can handle a good pack of nigras without much trouble. They'll fall in line when you give them the opportunity.

Now Chamberlain, the chief of all the thieving Republicans who'd been looting our state for eight years, stood up on the platform at the station to speak. He was a Yankee. A Harvard man.

Chamberlain tried and tried to give a speech, but we kept shouting him down. It wasn't long at all, with a little convincing from the armaments we displayed, that the nigra crowd shut up and let us run things. Every time Chamberlain tried to speak, we shut him up. After a while, we started calling for Smalls. Red Shirts were calling for the nigger to be killed. I thought for sure that was going to happen.

The Red Shirts started dispersing the Republicans who had showed up, scattering them off in all directions, leaving their leaders alone and in some danger up on the platform.

And then the platform itself started rocking. You should have seen fat old Smalls up on that platform, with his arms stuck straight out to the sides, and his eyes wide open as the stage wobbled.

The platform rocked and rocked. It was Red Shirts. They had five or six men under each support, and they started chanting in time, "Heave, heave, heave..." That platform rocked, the supports cracked, and the back of the platform started sinking towards the ground.

Well, Carpetbagger Chamberlain and Congressman Smalls skedaddled back inside the station. Quick as they could, they got on the train headed to Columbia.

A bunch of Red Shirts got on the train with them. I went along. I enjoyed being a part of that crowd. It was the first time in years, since the early years of the war, when the 13th Infantry was being mustered up, that I felt I was a part of something that was going somewhere. That does something to a man.

The Red Shirts gave Chamberlain and Smalls hell on the ride back to Columbia. They kept saying, "Well, ain't that Congressman Robert Smalls? Why that's the famous Congressman. I just want to ki----" They made it sound like they were going to say, "kill him," you see, but then they'd say, "I just want to kiss him. Don't you just want to kiss the Congressman?" they'd say to each other.

Smalls was no coward. He took it like a man. So did Chamberlain, for that matter. I didn't watch this part for very long. I never thought Smalls would make it back to Columbia alive on that train. I took him for a dead man.

The Wheelman

A letter from Major General Robert Smalls to Governor Daniel H. Chamberlain of South Carolina:

Beaufort, SC
Aug 24th 1876

To His Excellency
Governor DH Chamberlain
Columbia S.C.

Sir;

 I received a telegram from the Attorney General to call out the Militia, if necessary, to put down the riot on the Combahee. I proceeded yesterday to the disturbed rice districts and found no rioters, nor had there been a riot, but I did find a large body of men numbering about three hundred who had refused to work for checks, a sample of which you will find inclosed. The cause of the strike was that the rice Planters issued these checks instead of money, and that they are only redeemed in goods that must be purchased at exorbitant prices at the stores of the Planters, and the whole amount taken in goods, or change given in checks, thus making it impossible for the laborers to obtain any of the necessaries of life except through the Planters: and as these checks are payable in 1880 or at the pleasure of the Planter, other storekeepers will not receive them, nor will they buy medicines, or obtain the services of a physician in case of sickness.

Several of the strikers informed me that they had from five to ten dollars in checks and as yet had been unable to get money enough to pay their taxes.

The abolition of this check system will restore quiet satisfaction among the laborers in the rice districts of Beaufort and Colleton Counties, and I think it is due to them that some means be taken to protect them from the hardships that the check system involves. I am free to say that had the laborers been paid in money the rice fields would have been the most peaceful and orderly portion of the State.

I think you will agree with me, when I say that I wonder why these people have submitted to this imposition so long without murmuring, and that there is no class of laboring people in the United States that would have submitted so long without striking. In some respects the evils that have followed these checks are worse than the evils of slavery. The sure road to peace and contentment in the rice fields = good money for honest labor.

I found no lawless disposition among the strikers, many of them belonged to the Militia of the State and as such had arms, but not one of them appeared upon the ground with any kind of a weapon, except a club or a stick, saying that they knew it was against the law to bring their guns, but on the contrary I found from forty to sixty white men, mounted and armed with Spencer rifles sixteen shooters and double barreled shot guns; the presence of these armed white men did much to alarm and excite the strikers.

The strikers numbered about three hundred, and of this number warrants had been issued by Trial Justice Fuller for seven of them who were charged with whipping two men of their own number who had gone to work contrary to the agreement made by them in their club. No injury was done to property or violence offered to any but the two who had gone to work.

Upon going up to the strikers I asked those to come out of the crowd against whom warrants had been issued; no sooner had the request been made than the seven men gave themselves up;

they had previously objected to arrest by armed white men. The prisoners then went to Trial Justice Fuller's office and he not being at his office, at the request of the Sheriff they walked into Beaufort, fourteen miles distance, without a guard of any kind, and were in Beaufort hours before the arrival of the Sheriff.

At about 3 o'clock P.M. the entire crowd had dispersed and no signs of a strike being visible on the Combahee, the Planters having promised to pay cash once a week to the laborers. This was all they had asked.

I would suggest that Mr. Fuller the Trial Justice at Gardners Corner be removed as he is a large Planter, and one who issues checks to his laborers; therefore there must be naturally, dissatisfaction on the part of laborers when brought before him

I find on enquiry that the prices charged for goods where checks are taken are as follows grists 2.00 per bushel; regular price 1.00, bacon 25¢ per lb; regular price from 10 to 15¢ molasses 1.20 per gal regular price 40¢ and other articles in proportion.

Deputy Sheriff Sams acted in a very creditable manner, and is entitled to much credit for his coolness and bravery and the good judgement exercised in the discharge of his duty.

I hope you will be able through the Attorney General to adopt a remedy to cure the evils of the check system, and thus add to the peace of the rice districts and the prosperity of the laborer.

I am, Sir;

Very Respectfully

Robert Smalls

P.S. No Militia were needed, none were called for - Mr. Fuller was nine miles from the scene all the time.

Uncle Romulus

In the fall of 1876, a couple of months after Smalls was nearly killed in Edgefield, a few weeks after he wrote the letter above, the Red Shirts had their victory at the polls. Former Confederate General Wade Hampton, a Democrat, was elected Governor of South Carolina.

In the same election, Democratic candidate Samuel J. Tilden won the popular vote for President of the United States.

But Tilden was one vote short of defeating Republican Rutherford B. Hayes in the Electoral College. It fell to the U.S. House of Representatives to elect the President.

The vote in the House was deadlocked for months.

Eventually, the two parties compromised. Southern Democrats agreed to allow Hayes's election if he would withdraw Federal troops from the South.

Republican Robert Smalls (who had himself been reelected in the fall of 1876) argued vociferously against this move in the House of Representatives. He met personally with Hayes to beg him not to carry through with the deal, pleading that it would lead to widespread killing.

There is a large statue of Wade Hampton on the grounds of the Statehouse in Columbia, South Carolina. Hampton is astride a prancing horse, wearing his Confederate uniform, holding his hat humbly at his side.

I remember the statue from my frequent walks about the Statehouse grounds when I worked in the Governor's office. I had very little privacy in our cramped workspace inside the Statehouse. I would stroll around the Statehouse gardens to handle personal phone calls or just to get away from the backstabbing and plotting in the office.

My favorite statue on the statehouse grounds was the Strom Thurmond statue, its inscription amended (in those years) by permanent magic marker to include among his children his newly discovered African-American daughter. I also liked the imposing statue of Pitchfork Ben Tillman, a towering tribute to a butcher, with an inscription that makes him sound like a scoutmaster.

I remember the Hampton statue, though, because of the feverish conversation I had beside it once with Grace.

She had come to see me in my office. She was living in Columbia. I think she was enrolled in technical college there. It's hard to remember. It's so hard to remember the exact sequence of things with Grace. She lived for a while in Charleston. For a while in South Florida. For a while in Edgefield, South Carolina, for God's sake. There was the arts school. The tattoo artist. The former Navy Seal. I just can't keep it all straight.

Grace had come to the Statehouse that afternoon to see me, and I, realizing the conversation would be inconvenient in that political setting, took her out beside the large statue of Governor Wade Hampton for a talk.

Grace was so beautiful. Her long blond hair, tinged underneath with the red of her childhood, shone like a halo in the South Carolina sunlight. She was aware of the beauty. She fidgeted and flipped her hair for effect.

Borderline Personality Disorder brings an almost supernatural swinging of moods. The sufferer moves blithely from deep depression to flights of transport. Grace had recently returned from a particularly disastrous tour of Europe, financed by her grandparents. There she had fallen in love with a disturbed, wealthy Swede who violently beat her in Copenhagen. She escaped to the U.S. Embassy, a favor was called in with a U.S. Senator, and Grace was put on an expensive flight home.

Now she wanted to be a nurse, like her late mother, the one she had found with the top of her head blown off.

"But Uncle Rom," she was saying, "I can go to Midlands Tech and get my nursing degree in two years." This despite a lifetime of failing grades and near total lack of academic preparation.

"I'm turning my life around, this time," she said. "I've seen the light. I know the things I've been doing are wrong. I know the guys have been wrong. I know it all. I've always seen it all, really. I just couldn't stop myself from doing it.

"But this time I see the way out. I've got to let go and let God. If I just let God handle it, I've learned it all works out for the better. You know that."

I studied the multicolored pansies planted in the beds around the statue. I said nothing.

"Listen, it's like this painting I saw," Grace continued, "In Belgium, in Ghent, there's this painting in the cathedral. It's called the 'Lamb of God'. Have you ever seen it, Uncle Rom?"

My eyes stung.

How could she know that painting?

I had seen it twice in person. How could she be talking to me about it?

I dreamed about that painting for years.

I told her yes, I had seen it.

"I thought you would have!" Grace said. "I knew YOU would have seen it. You're so cool, Uncle Rom.

"In the middle," she said, "in the middle of it all- there's that lamb, there's that lamb standing on the altar with the blood gushing out of his chest and into the golden goblet..."

"*The Adoration of the Mystic Lamb*," I said.

"WhatEVER," Grace replied, laughing. "You would know it, of course. You're such a hopeless nerd! It's so incredible. The expression on the Lamb's face. It's just standing there, looking you straight in the eye, while the angels and all the world are gathered around worshiping it, and the blood is gushing in this fat stream out into that goblet, and the look on the Lamb's face..."

"I know," I said. "I've seen it."

"And you know," Grace said, "you just know this world we are living in is not the real one, that really all things are possible, and that all things work together ultimately for good, and that everyone, even people like me, can change and can live their lives in God's light."

I walked her around to the back side of Wade Hampton. She was manic now. I didn't want anyone coming out of the Statehouse to see me talking with her in that state.

"Uncle Rom," she laughed. "You don't have to hide me. You know everything I'm saying is true. It's the ultimate truth. I may completely mislead myself on so many things, but you know this is the truth."

"I know, Grace," I said. "I know."

The Good Neighbor

How did he become General Smalls, you ask? How did my rotund, jocular, half-Jewish neighbor become, of all things, a General?

It goes back to the late sixties, around the time he first became involved in politics. The Klu Klux Klan began to terrorize the Negro population. In Beaufort County, a place so overrun with Negroes that Senator Ben Tillman calls it "niggerdom," it was natural that a military force would be formed to take the field against the Klan.

A local militia headed by Robert Smalls was eventually made a part of the South Carolina State Militia by the Republican government. Within a couple of years, he was General Smalls.

Oh, the militia was delicious. They would meet on a Saturday at the armory, arm themselves to their pearly, white teeth with the most modern of rifles, and parade through the streets in their new, blue uniforms, with brass buckles and buttons gleaming in the sunlight. General Smalls had the best of the uniforms, and he would stride in front of the parade like the king he was.

Around the same time, Smalls organized his brass band. He called it the Allen Street Band. It had a set of uniforms more spectacular than the militia, with belts and buckles and buttons that were bigger and shinier and more audacious. The band members all had brass helmets, burnished until they glowed, topped with long, white egret feathers that swayed and vibrated as they marched.

We have enjoyed this band in the decades since. It plays at funerals, Fourth of July celebrations, the New Year. General Smalls brings them forth for the benefit and entertainment of the populace. You should see him stride at the head of that band as it marches down the street. He steps high, and his jowls pulsate to the music. He brandishes his sword as if it were a baton. He doesn't walk down the street with his band. He rolls down the street, throwing his ample belly from side to side.

And the Negroes love it. They line the route, dancing and clapping as the King of Beaufort County, the inimitable General Smalls, processes in his triumph, smiling as if the Lord God Almighty himself had placed him at the head of this joyful train of celebration.

The Wheelman

A speech by the Honorable Robert Smalls, Congressman from South Carolina, on the floor of the United States House of Representatives, February 24, 1877:

As a Representative of the State of South Carolina, I rise to submit my views regarding the investigation of the election by a committee of this House. The unfortunate division existing among the people of my State as to who is the lawfully elected governor of the State and who were the lawfully elected presidential electors has led to this investigation. I am happy to say the committee is unanimous in their conclusion that the Hayes electors received a majority of the votes cast and I regret to have to add that they are divided politically upon the governorship.

Under ordinary circumstances I would be content to allow the report of the committee to go upon the record with no further opposition than to record my vote against the majority report, believing, as I do, that the report of a partisan committee cannot and will not be accepted by the people of my State as an honest conclusion based upon the results of the investigation. The committee having divided upon the important question of who is the legally elected governor, the question remains an open one, to be accepted or denied according to party opinion.

I therefore propose at this time to submit to this House and the American people, in as concise shape as possible, the facts relating to the late political campaign and election in my State. The Democratic party pursued a policy calculated to drive from the State every white man who affiliated with the Republican party or who would refuse to join them in their attempts to deprive the Negro of the rights guaranteed him by the Constitution of South Carolina and of the United States, the manifest intention being to reduce the Negro to a condition of political dependence upon the former slaveholder; to place him in the power of the men who had degraded his manhood, who had reduced him to a condition of ignorance through centuries of enforced subjection. The Democratic party adhered to such a policy with these results: they committed large numbers of murders, resorted to violence and outrages, and terrorized entire counties. Thus, the political rights of 10,000 Negroes and access to the ballot box were denied by means of fraud.

The white race of the South possesses intelligence and courage. The existence of the institution of slavery cemented their personal interests and compelled them to act in concert in political matters. The relation of master to slave produced in the ruling class a domineering spirit, a disposition to ignore and trample down the rights of those they could not control. They became in a large degree cruel, refusing education to and ignoring the sanctity of the family relations of their slaves; they assumed the slave had no rights and denied the fact of his being a brother man and entitled to his personal liberty. They never learned to recognize such a principle and would tolerate no free expression of opinion. Such qualities provoked the late civil strife between the North and the South, and are today responsible for the unhappy condition of the South. The late slaveholding class will not submit peacefully to a government they cannot control, believing they are a superior race; and, not recognizing the rights of the colored man, they feel justified in resorting to any means or power to accomplish their end. To achieve their purpose they take human life with impunity, drive citizens from their homes, and perpetrate fraud against them.

Such is the policy and character of the men who, having disgraced the name of South Carolina by their acts, now ask to be sustained in the result accomplished. On the other hand, the Negro race, under ordinary circumstances is gentle, patient and affectionate; possessed of no cruel impulses, they are a harmless race, generous to a fault; their confidence is easily won. These qualities are the outgrowth of long years of suffering and have become engrafted in their natures by the bitter lessons of experience. The granting of suffrage to them originated a new and controlling element in the Southern States. This, Mr. Speaker, has led to all the sorrows and the cruelties they have felt in the last ten years. The determination of the former slaveholding class to control them has prompted the many scenes of cruelty that make the history of the new South one of blood and form the subject for one of the darkest pages in American history. The blood of the innocent freedman, shed by southern democrats, will in the future prove to be one of the dark spots upon the fair name of the American Republic.

It is manifest that two political elements so widely different in their character would provoke much antagonism, but I do not think it ever entered the mind of the most apprehensive that the white race would resort to such inhuman brutality to recover power. If the Negroes had been as a race their equals in courage there might possibly be some palliation for so inhuman a policy, but when it was considered their cruelty was against a harmless race, it affords no defense, and their course becomes the blacker in comparison with their boasted chivalry, their claim of superior gentleness, and of those virtues which adorn the human race. The oppressed colored race can ask no greater punishment upon their persecutors than to call the attention of the civilized world to the history of the South for the last ten years, and to a comparison of the manner by which a rebellious people were treated by a generous Government, and in turn the treatment of the Negro race by the pardoned class, and they challenge the annals of civilization to show a people who have maintained a more peaceful policy under such trying circumstances.

Uncle Romulus

We imagine now the scene in Beaufort, where Congressman Smalls has come during the recess of the United States House of Representatives. The large, white policemen stride onto the porch of Smalls's stately, Prince Street home. They are dressed in ill-fitting, woolen suits. They are armed with the writ. They are armed with whiteness. They are armed with the might of law.

Smalls rises to meet them. He is blackness. His nappy hair is matted. His suit is immaculate. It fits his rotundity with tailored precision. He offers his hands.

The black crowd has gathered in the neighborhood. They already know what is to happen.

The buzz of threat pulsates through the crowd. Smalls, with a nod, denies them the right to interfere.

His wrists are locked in the steel cuffs.

The neighbors watch. The crowd watches.

The wheelman of the *Planter* is captured and chained. The people have their hero plucked from their midst. They are confused.

With a dirgeful cadence, the leader of the Allen Street Band strides, hands chained, from his house to the waiting carriage.

He is taken to the train station. A few gloating members of the press follow. The uppity nigger is chained. The tailored jacket is bunched at the shoulders. The slave is going back to massah.

The passengers on the train recoil. The Negro has been caught. Did he rape a white woman? Did he ransack the house? Did he leer and rob and lurk in the bushes and hide in the woodpile and loll in his greed and rapacity? Now he, as they all ultimately must be, is brought around to the natural order of things. He must be chained, incarcerated, broken, trained, subdued, lynched, killed, shot, whipped. Such is the way of the Universe.

Smalls rides all day on the train, his hands cuffed. He is surrounded by the fat, white policemen. He is still uppity. He does not cower. He does not duck. He does not bob. He does not say, "Yassuh."

He is the General. He is the Congressman.

In the evening, the train stops in Columbia, and they emerge to a rainy, South Carolina winter. The majority of the onlookers are black. The minority are white. All know the drill. There is a moment when they stare, and then, almost immediately, they look away. The Negro is chained, but what if he breaks loose? What if he sees them staring? It is as if they are watching a chained lion being led through their midst. Thank God for the chains. Thank God for the policemen, or he might come for them. Black or white, they recoil at the thought.

Then someone recognizes Smalls. There are few photographs at the time, and few ways to distribute them widely. Yet someone would have seen him before, speaking from the stump. Speaking in the Legislature. One would recognize him by sight. They would all know his name.

"That's General Bob Smalls!" someone will say, and the word will spread among the onlookers, as he is led to the waiting carriage.

Now the majority, the black ones, will change their minds. Now their hero is led before them. He is to be placed amongst the thieves. Why must this be done?

But they know already. It is the natural order of things. Things are being placed right side up. The world has been upside down, but now it will be restored to wholeness and unity and reconciliation. General Hampton prances upon his horse, and General Smalls is to be displayed among the thieves and receive the punishment. This punishment must come. It is right and good. It is what is deserved. He will suffer for his people.

Ain't he the one been running Beaufort County like he was king?

Uncle Romulus

In contemplating my Negro ancestry, we should consider, perhaps, the case of Sally Hemmings and her children. Sally Hemmings was the slave concubine of President Thomas Jefferson, founder of the Republic. He had several Negro children by her, who were denied by his white descendants and generations of historians. The denial persisted for nearly two centuries, until DNA testing established a high likelihood of truth in the story that had spread as scandal during his presidency.

Beautiful Sally was the half-sister of Jefferson's late wife, but she was a generation younger. When Jefferson was widowed and serving as Ambassador to France, Sally arrived in Paris as a traveling companion to his white daughter (who was also Sally's half-niece).

In Post-Revolutionary France, Sally was free as soon as she stepped off the ship. She could no longer be held by the slave laws of Virginia. Her brother, Jefferson's cook, was in Paris already with the Ambassador. Sally's brother was being trained as a French chef.

The widowed Jefferson, author of the Declaration of Independence, was forty-six at the time. Jefferson's wife had inherited Sally when her (and Sally's) father died.

Jefferson then inherited Sally when his wife died. Sally, of course, was also his sister-in-law.

When Jefferson returned to the United States from Paris two years later, Sally was expecting. She could have stayed in Paris and been free. She returned to Virginia with Jefferson to be his slave and bear his slave children.

In all, Sally had six children, four of whom survived to adulthood. Most historians now believe these children were fathered by Jefferson. That has not always been the case. Although there were published news accounts of Jefferson's black children during his lifetime, throughout the intervening history of the United States most historians have held these news accounts to be mere fabrications by Jefferson's political enemies, not to be believed at all.

But now- now that we have a mulatto President of the United States, most historians believe Jefferson was indeed the father.

Jefferson was planting the European seed in this African line at almost exactly the same time my ancestor was injecting the African seed into the lily-white Welsh line of my forebears.

As Jefferson's black children came to maturity, Jefferson saw to their eventual freedom.

He simply allowed the elder two, a boy and a girl, to leave Monticello one day in a carriage. They proceeded, apparently with their father's blessing, to Washington, DC, where tradition maintains they entered white society, married well, prospered, and disappeared into white America. Their descendants have been lost to changing names and the need to forget their secret blackness. No one knows where they are or what they are called. These two children of Sally eventually stopped responding to their Negro siblings' mail, and the family lost all contact with them.

Jefferson freed the younger black Jeffersons in his will. After his death, they remained in Charlottesville until their mother died some years later. After Sally died, about the time my family tree recovers from its undocumented hiatus between the Pee Dee and Charleston, these two younger children moved to Chillicothe, Ohio, where they lived in a mixed-race community, recognized as mulattoes.

In 1852, one of those two children, Eston Hemmings, moved with his mixed-race wife to Madison, Wisconsin. When they arrived in Wisconsin, they changed their last name to Jefferson and entered Madison's white community.

Eston's son, John Wayles Jefferson, was a contemporary of my great, great grandfather, the Redshirt and officer in the 13th South Carolina Infantry. John Wayles Jefferson served in the Union army during the war. He was a more accomplished officer than my ancestor. John Wayles Jefferson rose to the rank of Colonel in command of the Wisconsin 8th Infantry. The Wisconsin 8th served in the West, fighting at Vicksburg and Nashville and Memphis, among many other places. John Wayles Jefferson never would have come into contact with the 13th South Carolina or its part-Negro lieutenant, my great, great grandfather.

During the war, Colonel Jefferson ran into a former neighbor from Chillicothe, Ohio. As soon as possible, Colonel Jefferson pulled the man aside and explained that no one in his regiment was aware of his Negro ancestry, and he would greatly appreciate it if his former neighbor and friend could keep that a secret. The man gladly obliged this request, it is reported.

Colonel Jefferson never married and had no recognized children. One of his siblings' descendant, a white man living in California in 1998, was the man who volunteered to have his DNA tested, along with a descendant of Jefferson's acknowledged, white children. The results of this DNA test established the likelihood that President Thomas Jefferson, was, in fact, the father of Sally Hemings' children, and thus the grandfather of Colonel John Wayles Jefferson.

My own story of mixed-race ancestry is not so unusual, then. Published studies claim that some twenty percent of those Americans who self-identify as white in fact have some African ancestry. And roughly seventy percent of those who identify themselves as black have European ancestors. What a long history we have struggled to forget.

So- when the African seed was reinjected into my family line in the 21st Century, you can see a great deal of cultural and historical weight lay behind the events that followed.

The Great, Great

I see the nigra Smalls has been arrested down in Beaufort and is charged with accepting a bribe as a state Senator. You never can tell about people. I wouldn't really have expected it. I disagree with his politics, but based on the way he handled himself at the rally in Edgefield and on the train ride back to Columbia, I took him as a more solid man.

My daddy told me all politicians were crooks. Maybe he was right.

I'm no fool. If Robert Smalls is a crook, then is General Wade Hampton a crook? You don't want to think it, but what is a General except a politician? Of course, if you're following that line of reasoning, what about Robert E. Lee? Or General Washington? You don't really want to go there, do you?

But you've got General Grant, who turned out to be a real embarrassment of a crook once he got into politics.

It's a messy business. Best to stay out of it, I suppose. I wonder what will come of this man Smalls.

The Jurist

The man is brought before me, and I am to judge. All has been arranged. The jury has been selected. The jury has been paid. There are sufficient Negroes bought to assure the correct verdict.

The witness has been suborned. The gallery has gathered. The press are here. I have donned my robe and mounted the bench, and now I must play the role.

The outcome is rarely so well arranged in advance, but this is what I do. I don the robe. I don the manner. I choose the words. I speak in stentorian tones. I scowl or listen with wise, indifferent expression. This is what I do.

How rarely do I actually apply the law? How often am I simply an actor on a stage, giving the proceeding gravitas and meaning? I am like a priest in my robe, moving across the front of the courtroom as the priest moves across the chancel at communion, dancing the prearranged, expected dance, making the motions and mouthing the words that so comfort the congregation. The priest does what is expected. The judge does what is expected. This gives comfort and peace. We have danced the dance of the universe. We dance out the will of the Almighty. We move in our preordained circles, doing nothing that is of any real significance, but the dance itself is of all significance, of all importance. For we are dancing the deep unfolding of life. We are doing what will be done. Thy will be done, on earth as it is in heaven.

The accused stands before me. His innocence or guilt is irrelevant. His sins (and we know, of course, that he has sinned- no innocent man has ever stood before me) his sins may not be relevant to the charges at all. His sin is theft, for sure. He stole a Confederate ship. He stole himself. He stole his wife. He stole other men's property. He stole our pride.

He is accused of theft of public trust, of bribery. My goodness, what politician in Columbia is not guilty of that sin? This is the sure charge. There can be no doubt. Sweep through the streets. Seine the public houses. Bring them all in, the elected. They are all guilty. There is no doubt.

Yet this man stands here as if he were innocent. Oh, come now. Wouldn't they all stand there with that look? The irreverence. The defiance. The indignation. "I, an elected one? How can you accuse me?" Like a Presbyterian before the seat of Judgment.

Yes, this witness they have produced is a weasel. Really, could they not come up with someone better? The scoundrel oozes deceit.

Has he ever said an honest word in his life? He reads from his secret book, written in secret code, he claims, that no one else can decipher. Oh, it IS rich. It IS so delicious. If this pack of thieves is going to accuse one of the elect, it IS delightful to see such a ridiculous story laid out.

But I must maintain the show. I must stay in character. I must dance the dance. We must move toward the inevitable, the preordained.

The jurors sit with vapid faces. What is it to live in such ignorance, such prejudice and stupid faith, so devoid of hope and imagination they can be bought for a song, be fed a ridiculous feast of lies, and then be counted on to deliver their own hero to his condemnation? God save us from a jury of our peers.

For his part, Smalls is doing the dance awfully well. I love his suit of clothes. How MUCH did the man pay for such elegance? Surely he is on the take. He sits in earnest outrage. How DARE they? He is so above the weasel in the witness chair. He looks as if he would spit on the weasel if such a man ever dared to speak to him directly.

Who knows the truth in such matters? I've been doing this long enough to know the truth is rarely revealed to us in ways we can understand. How often, in those trials where I sat disinterested, the outcome intriguingly NOT preordained, have I watched the weight of truth waft back and forth between the antagonists? I fear truth may simply be withheld from us mortals.

But judge I must. It is my destiny. It is my role.

The stories must be told. That is what the attorneys do. They tell a story. They take the truth, the lies, the imagination, the outrageous, the laughably false, they take it all, and they dance with it. They do their dance as I do mine. I see them in my mind's eye wheeling like dervishes in front of the jury, dancing their stories into being.

And so we take the testimony of this weasel, the scoundrel no one would ever believe if he spoke to them face-to-face, and we dance it into the most wonderful of tales. I wouldn't be surprised if the tale weren't far from the real truth. How did Smalls get to be so rich? What has he ever done but steal a ship and hold public office? Really now. He lorded it about this town like a king. God knows how he's been prancing around Washington.

But he maintains his innocence. He sits in outraged dignity. His attorneys assail the obvious as they attack the witness. The witness's credibility. My God! As if the word "credibility" could be used in the same sentence in which this man is referenced. It IS laughable. But the outcome is preordained. I must make my rulings, and the dance must be danced.

The jurors, in their imbecility, must feign objectivity and honesty before they render their verdict. With no practice and experience are they aware of the expressions they must display as they listen to the proceedings? I watch them. They, of course, are not aware. They look more weaselly than the bloody witness himself. God help us.

And, so, when the dance is all done, and the newspapers have made up their stories and printed them, and the attorneys have twisted everything, and the jury has adjourned to ponder the inevitable, and they have returned with their preordained verdict, it is now time for me to render the judgment that has been arranged.

The defendant Smalls rises. I judge him.

And then, it is really most remarkable. He stands there and stares me in the face.

He stares at me for a full minute. There is silence in the courtroom. He stares me full in the face, as if he were my father looking at me. I cannot meet his stare. I turn away, but I cannot rise and leave.

This man is the most uppity nigger in history. He stares me full in the face as if I knew better my whole life. As if he were in the right and I were in the wrong. As if this bit of theater we have put on for the benefit of the citizens of South Carolina were anything other than a bit of theater. As if the truth were there, plain for us all to see, and he could actually see it himself. As if he were a seer of the truth in a world full of blind men.

The bloody audacity.

Uncle Romulus

It's time now to talk about the arc of the moral universe.

Purported arc of the purportedly moral purported universe. Posited by Dr. King, inspired by Theodore Parker. My students are mystified by what King said. They do not understand it.

"The arc of the moral universe is long," King said, "but it bends toward justice."

This seems to me to pose the ultimate question.

The particular sub-arc covered in our story starts in Russia with Leo Tolstoy. Let me try now to trace out that sub-arc, from Tolstoy to Ghandi to King, and then I'll tell you how Robert Smalls ties in.

Let us start by considering the writings of Smalls's contemporary Leo Tolstoy. Tolstoy's novels and stories tell of many Russian serfs and former serfs, many masters and former masters, their living conditions, their relationships, their hopes and dreams and foibles and heartbreaks, their damnations, salvations, and deaths. Leo Tolstoy was a slave owner as a young man. Before he married, he fathered a child by one of his serfs.

Tolstoy witnessed in his lifetime the freeing of those slaves. In the decades that followed, Tolstoy became a very religious man, a spiritual leader.

Later in life, Tolstoy wrote a book titled *The Kingdom of God is Within You*. Mohandis K. Ghandi read *The Kingdom of God is Within You*, not long after it was translated into English, and he started up a correspondence with Count Tolstoy in the final year of the Russian sage's life. In their correspondence, the two men discussed their evolving ideas on non-violence. Ghandi later credited Tolstoy with inspiring his own doctrine of non-violence as expounded in *Indian Home Rule*.

And, of course, Ghandi's ideas inspired Martin Luther King, Jr..

And Martin Luther King ended the ethnic cleansing campaign that Wade Hampton and Pitchfork Ben Tillman had set in motion almost a century before in South Carolina.

In May of 2012, a panel discussion was held in Charleston, South Carolina on the life and times of Robert Smalls. It was hosted by Smalls's great, great grandson and featured a panel of distinguished historians. The panel discussion was broadcast on the C Span television network. As of this writing, a video of the discussion is still available on the Internet. The discussion is fascinating. Smalls's life story in the larger context of the history of race in America is so weighty. And that story has been so thoroughly suppressed for such a long time.

The video becomes a bit more poignant as its moderator, Smalls's urbane, Duke-educated, great, great grandson, tries to have patience with some of the audience who rise to pose questions to the panel. The brothers (he calls them that) just can't seem to bring themselves to the point.

So Smalls's great, great grandson tries to save the question-and-answer period by addressing the panel of historians himself. Could you, he asks, help us understand Robert Smalls's influence and significance in the late 1800's by comparing him to a 20th- or 21st-Century figure with whom we are familiar?

A great question, but one which stumps the panel. They ponder. No answer is forthcoming.

Smalls's great, great grandson waits an uncomfortable while and then moves them on to another question. And later, as that question is being answered, one of the panel members, a bookish, balding, white historian, asks if he can return to the question about the 20th-Century person who was most like Smalls.

After much thought, he says, he thinks the best comparison would be Dr. Martin Luther King, Jr.

There is silence in the assembly.

My God, this is the King he's talking about. This is the sainted Dr. King, the greatest American who ever lived, the man who changed our whole world without shedding any blood but his own.

The historian went on to make a thoughtful case for why Smalls could be compared to Dr. King. One point he made: Smalls stood up in the constitutional convention of 1895 and went toe-to-toe with Pitchfork Ben Tillman. Ben Tillman was an acknowledged murderer of African-Americans. Smalls, the historian said, was a man of unparalleled courage in the face of injustice, just like Dr. King.

Marshall Evans

I wonder where the arc of the moral universe is bending. Will Tolstoy's (and Ghandi's, and King's) dreams of a society based on non-violence and justice ever come to pass?

Let's face it, the past really shouldn't hurt us any more, should it? But the stories we tell ourselves about the past just might shape the future as we travel along the arc.

The Great, Great

So I read in the papers that Smalls is convicted by a jury made up largely of his fellow Negroes. Moreover, I read he never did really steal the *Planter*. He made up the story and told it to the Northern papers when he got to Hilton Head. Another slave piloted the *Planter* out of the harbor while Smalls hid below in the hold. It looks like the man was a complete fraud.

And all I can say is thank God Almighty for General Wade Hampton. And thank God Ben Tillman got me involved with the Red Shirts. Maybe we will make something of this state for my children and their children and their children's children. I would hate to think what we might have left them.

It's like my family. If there's a colored past to it, the only way to move on for your sake and your children's sake is to put it behind you. The past is the past, and you can't do anything to change it.

Uncle Romulus

So how did the African seed come again into my family line? As you might expect, the opportunity was offered by Grace.

Young men quickly discovered troubled, beautiful Grace. There was a depressing string of them. There were some really bad ones.

Her cousins and friends tried to intervene. They tried to save her. Again and again. And then they began to give up.

Shortly after I was released from the mental hospital, Grace called and asked me to go on a walk with her. It was an invitation I cherished. She was checking on me. My suicidal impulses were largely gone. I was in counseling and on prescription drugs to treat the anxiety, and the treatment was working.

Grace led me on a loop through the cemetery, past her mother's grave, right next to where Grace's own grave would soon be. We didn't stop there. Grace didn't dwell on it. How could she keep up her chipper, beautiful conversation?

She wanted to talk about boys. There was this boy. She was serious about him, she said. I could tell he thought he was sleeping with the town slut. She wanted to know how to make him a real boyfriend.

In my heart, I knew it wasn't possible. But she was so full of hope. And she was so full of love, so much the little girl who had bounced through our house with our daughters and jumped and played and cuddled with us all on the sofa as we watched *The Little Mermaid*.

There was all this hope shining out. And I was buying it and believing it, and I did my best with the conversation. I was trying to lead her in some direction that might help. I was the uncle who had been married for decades. I was the stable one.

Oh, what drug-fueled self-delusion! Here was a desperately mentally-ill young woman, a recent survivor of the suicide of her mother, walking through the same cemetery where that mother was buried, in her own way trying to talk her uncle out of suicide by pretending to be something she definitely wasn't- a love-struck, innocent teenager.

And I was pretending to be something I wasn't: a stable, decent uncle who could show her the way.

Or was all this pretending closer to the truth than it appears on the surface? I don't really know. I am genuinely unsure.

Uncle Romulus

The question of Robert Smalls's guilt, decided by a predominately African-American jury of his peers, has never really been settled. People take the trial and make of it what they will. The only witness against Smalls was a convicted felon. This man claimed he paid Smalls five-thousand-dollars in exchange for a government printing contract. That witness's testimony, filled with contradictions, was skillfully impugned by Smalls's attorneys. The witness read from what he claimed was a diary written in a code known only to him.

Smalls biographers, especially the authors of the three academic biographies published since 1970, comb meticulously through the trial, so there is really no need to do so here.

It is more convenient nowadays that Smalls be wrongly accused and wrongly convicted. For the century or so before 1970, it was more convenient that Smalls be a crook. Historical judgment is currently shifting toward innocence, and I, on the whole, tend to agree with that direction. The trial was clearly cooked up and orchestrated by the Wade Hampton government.

Afterwards, Smalls claimed a messenger from Governor Hampton offered to drop the charges and pay him ten thousand dollars if he would step down from his seat in Congress.

Smalls claimed this envoy admitted the Democrats held no personal hostility toward Smalls. They felt Smalls had always treated white people fairly and honestly. But, according to Smalls, the envoy said, "We must have this government. We will have this government."

Smalls's story is entirely self-serving, and there is no independent corroboration. But how would there be any independent confirmation of this story? Smalls was either an honest man, one of the most honest men in South Carolina politics, or he was an inveterate liar and self-promoter.

Or he was something else. He might have been something else. It's possible all of us are altogether something else, and we rarely realize it.

The Mystery

We done tek Bob Smalls an we done showuh he with grace. Finely he bandon he seff into ow hand. We break he den. We break he like a sack official lamb.

He ow beloved. We be well pleased.

We mos specially like when he steppin front of dat band.

The Governor

The Negro Smalls is a most difficult case. We took him under our control and broke him. We broke him completely. We had him handcuffed, led from his home. We jailed him. We tried him. We had him convicted. We offered him absolution, if he would merely renounce the madness in which he had been engaged.

But it did not work with Smalls. Instead, he became another man.

One thing we have learned, from all our years of struggle, is that all men have their breaking point. You command men by taking them to the breaking point. You learn how to find that point, you lay out what will be required to get the man to that point, and you apply it.

Most will see the breaking point coming, and they will bend to your will before you have to take them there. Others must be taken all the way.

We had tried again and again to show Smalls his breaking point. The man cared nothing for his own life, and he carried on in spite of the clear threats to his continued existence.

In the end, we decided that killing him would simply make a martyr, and a more promising approach materialized. We decided to destroy his integrity.

When I heard of his reaction to his trial, I knew we had him.

He was sentenced to three years at hard labor. I never had any intention of having him serve that. The bargain had been made at a national level. Imprisoning one of their heroes was never really an option. So his appeal, his release during his appeal, and his eventual pardon were inevitable.

What was not inevitable, or at least not predictable, was that he did not desist. Instead, he simply became more defiant. It was as if the man were infused with the spirit.

We had him. In every public confrontation for the rest of his life, he would be the convicted bribe taker. Yet he continued to stand up in public, stand up in elections, stand up in Congress, for God's sake, as if he were a man who should be listened to. It was remarkable, and, while it was a heartrending spectacle, there was an enchanting mystery to it.

I don't think anyone will remember Robert Smalls in the future. He will be forgotten like all the other Negroes who took their moment of power and glory after the war. We will write the history, and we will set the story straight.

The thing I will remember about that man was what he did after we broke him. It really was the most extraordinary thing. The greatest of deeds pass away and are remembered by no one. No monument is built, no story is written, the memories fade and die with the rememberers. But quiet deeds that are testaments to courage are the real substance of life.

The Good Neighbor

After a brief hiatus in which he dealt with his legal troubles, my Jewish neighbor stood for Congress again. I can pinpoint this memory to 1880, around the birth of my first grandchild. I remember Smalls coming over to my front porch to congratulate us. His wife Hannah, hunched a bit with age, reached out to my daughter for the child. My daughter betrayed a momentary look of terror. She glanced to me for guidance.

By this time, I must admit, I loved the man. It was, I think, his high-stepping, rolling, fat-bellied marching at the head of his band that won me over, just as it won over the crowds of shimmying darkies who lined the streets to watch him.

Smalls told me at the presentation of my grandson, as Hannah cuddled and kissed the baby, that he was standing for Congress again, his pardon having come from Governor Hampton before the U.S. Supreme Court even heard his appeal.

Smalls's Democratic opponent was George Tillman, the elder brother of Senator Tillman, the pitchfork man. I never much cared for the Senator, but I met George a couple of times and saw him speak in public more than once. George struck me as a rather dignified and decent sort. He only represented our district a short while. After the Democrats tangled with Bob Smalls, they carved Beaufort County out of Tillman's district, so he wouldn't have to run against the King of Beaufort County again.

I rode with the King to a political rally in Gillisonville that fall. Rather I followed him on the train, sitting at a distance from him, really. Even this decision was most imprudent, I later found to my dismay. It showed me what was really happening to Negroes in South Carolina politics.

In Gillisonville, there was a crowd of about a hundred coloreds gathered to listen to Smalls when he arrived. No white person would have publicly claimed to support Robert Smalls by that time in South Carolina. I surely wouldn't have done so, and I was his friend and neighbor.

As Smalls prepared to talk, the audience began to swell. Colored men and women came walking down the street to join the meeting.

The scene was peaceful and pleasant. But then a group of some dozen white men, wearing red shirts, came galloping into town on their horses, whooping a loud, rebel yell.

The lead red shirts started knocking the hats off the colored men in the streets. I watched as two white men leaned over in their saddles and slapped the faces of colored girls.

The riders shouted at Smalls and demanded they be allowed to hold a joint political meeting, Democrats and Republicans.

Now, those were different times. The colored folk still had some fight in them. They didn't take this by cowering and shuffling away as they would now. The colored men were angry. They spoke of getting their guns and fighting back.

Smalls wouldn't let them. He herded them into a nearby store, insisting they could have a civil conversation in there. I remained outside, not daring to identify myself with the Negroes. I could see Smalls beginning his stump speech inside. In a matter of minutes, he had calmed his people.

But the white Red Shirts escalated the incident. One of them, a tall, rangy lad barely a man, began firing his pistol at the side of the store. Women inside the store screamed and wailed. The Red Shirts called for torches to burn the store. They had the place surrounded. No one could have run out of the building without coming directly into the Red Shirts' line of fire.

I was in a hot sweat. I had come to Gillisonville to watch my neighbor give a political speech. I expected a funny speech like you might hear at a colored funeral or in the back of one of their churches. It's entertaining. We all love to hear it and chuckle.

But now I believed I was going to witness the murder of these poor people. I was too scared to intervene. I was too attached to leave. I remember the sweat pouring under my shirt. I remember the panic I felt.

The only thing that saved those people's lives, I am convinced, was the sound of gunshots coming down the road from out of town. Colored men, alerted by the ruckus, had gathered up guns of their own and were marching toward the town, firing warning shots.

The Red Shirts considered standing to fight. Quite a number of them wanted to stay and start killing. But more level-headed leadership prevailed. The Red Shirts mounted their horses and galloped out of town, shouting promises to be back on election day and kill any nigger they saw at the polls.

I stood on the street corner like a man drained. The armed colored men continued to pour into town. If I weren't accompanying Robert Smalls, I don't know what would have become of me. It is entirely reasonable to think I might have been killed myself.

When it came time to leave, we learned the Red Shirts had merely repositioned themselves aboard the train to wait for Smalls. I boarded the train and took my seat expecting to see a murder. The Red Shirts paid me no attention. I was not associated with Smalls in their minds. Anticipation made me sick to my stomach. I thought I would vomit.

The train left the station and returned to Beaufort without incident.

My neighbor had slipped into the baggage car in the darkness and rode there to avoid the attention of the Red Shirts.

This memory is repulsive to me. Politics is a filthy thing. Politics in South Carolina is as filthy as politics gets.

Uncle Romulus

He started calling himself Bobby Large. He posed as a rapper, a buster of rhymes, a minstrel of injustice, a messiah of cool. He was, in reality, a poor, fat, black kid in Upstate South Carolina at the dawn of the 21st Century.

I don't know why Bobby Lewson decided to start doing this. I had introduced him to Robert Smalls in response to his essay on Faulkner, and Bobby was fascinated by Smalls's story. He wanted to write an essay about Smalls for class, but there was no way I could work the subject into any of the essay assignments we were forced to give in Freshman Lit. He wrote an essay anyway, largely researched from Wikipedia, but charged with a real admiration for the 19th-Century hero, I thought. I couldn't give him any class credit for it. It didn't fit in with the syllabus. I even asked the

Department Head if I could do anything to reward Bobby's initiative and passion. She said my hands were tied. She looked like I had made her suck on a lemon.

Sometime after that, Bobby started calling himself Bobby Large. I remember laughing with him about it the first time I heard. But I'm not really sure he meant it as a joke.

Bobby made a D for the semester, which was not high enough to transfer to a real college, so he had to repeat the course, and we got to be friends that second semester. Bobby was a kid looking for a way to succeed. I got the impression he really didn't come from too bad a family background. He mentioned his mother. She seemed to have some standing in the community.

It all led me to a smug, self-congratulatory, warm feeling every time Bobby Large walked out of my office after a conversation. Here was this kid, with all the impediments our society placed in front of him, and he would stop by to see me, without my having to call. We would talk about things. And he seemed to care. And I cared. I think I really did care, as much as I could allow myself to do so, because things almost never worked out for these kids. At least not in college.

But I felt good about this one. I felt like I was doing the right thing. I so often had this nagging feeling in my gut that I wasn't doing the right thing. But Bobby made me feel better about it all.

It all felt fine, that is, until I happened to drive by the ThruWay Lounge near the center of our small town one Friday afternoon. There on the sidewalk, in front of the beer joint, I saw Grace hanging from Bobby Large's neck.

Marshall Evans

As I drove by in my BMW, doing my best not to turn and look, doing my very best to pretend I didn't see, Grace's hand clutched at Bobby Large's crotch, tugging at Bobby's oversized pants.

Grace ducked her golden hair beneath the brim of his ridiculous goddamn nigger cap, and she nibbled on his ear.

The Yankee Paper

Boston Daily Globe, May 13, 1882, front page, above the fold:

THE COLOR LINE IN BOSTON

Excitement Over the Refusal to Accommodate General Smalls at the Revere, Presumably on Account of His Color- An Interview with the Ex-Congressman- Explanation by the Proprietor of the Hotel.

General Robert Smalls, ex-member of Congress from South Carolina, arrived from Washington yesterday. General Smalls, who is a colored gentleman, will be remembered as having captured the steamer *Planter* in Charleston harbor in 1863. During the night he ran her into the Union lines, and for this act he was made a general by order of the United States government. He is now contesting the seat in Congress occupied by G. D. Tillman. The general was met at the depot by a committee from the Shaw Guard Veterans Association and escorted to the Revere House, where, it is stated, the committee had engaged rooms some days ago. When they arrived at the hotel it is said that the parties in the office disappeared, and the general and his friends waited some time, during which it is alleged that no one recognized them. They finally saw a clerk, and to him stated the object of their visit. The clerk told them, it is said, that all the rooms were filled. The party then referred to the fact that rooms had been engaged a few days before for General Smalls but no satisfactory answer was obtained. The party then re-entered their carriages and went to the Quincy House, where they were accommodated. A call at Room 10, Quincy House, last evening, found the general, who in reply to queries said:

"I left Washington, D.C. at 1:30 p.m. yesterday and arrived here at 8 o'clock this morning, and must say I was a little surprised at the reception I met with at the Revere House. When I left my carriage a porter took my valise and carried it into the hotel, but when the clerk saw me he slipped away. Another, however, came in and informed me that they could not accommodate me, giving as a reason that their house was being painted, and that everything was upside down. I thought this rather a strange proceeding, owing to the fact that the committee informed me that they had engaged rooms for me the day previous. However, I took the situation in at a glance, and, like the Irishman, says I to myself: 'When my friends engaged the rooms they thought that General Smalls was a white man; but when they

Saw He Was Colored

some excuse was necessary and they gave a good one.

"To tell the truth I do not think that were I to resort to the 'civil rights bill' I would have any chance of action. In fact I am satisfied that they were all turned upside down, but you know that perhaps were I of the Caucasian race they might have squeezed me in somehow. I am satisfied, however, with my apartments here. You see here there are in the dining-room say thirty or forty tables. I can go to one table by myself and sit down, and parties who object to sitting with a colored man have plenty of seats at other tables. Now in Washington I stay at a private house, but the line is not drawn there at the leading hotels between the races as here. Now there is Pinchback from Louisiana. When he and his family are in Washington they stay at Willard's and like their meals at the same table with other senators, members of Congress, etc. But I am satisfied. I leave tomorrow evening for Washington, where, after a short stay, I will

Take a Trip Home

to Beauford and then return to Washington and prosecute what I deem my just rights against Mr. Tillman."

The general is 43 years of age, a good and fluent speaker, and well posted on matters appertaining to his native State. In bidding adieu to the writer he said: "You can say I like Massachusetts and hope to return again shortly. My daughter graduated at West Newton, where she made many warm friends, and where I will, if possible, visit tomorrow."

Mr. Charles H. Perrin, proprietor of the Revere House, says that on Thursday some parties called at his hotel for the purpose of engaging rooms for General Smalls, and that they were informed that owing to the condition of his house they could not give a decided answer as to whether or not they would have a room; that the room they claimed as being engaged, No. 31, was being painted and upset (a visit by the reporter fully verified this); that after General Smalls had left he had to refuse rooms to several of his old patrons; and that the idea of Smalls being a colored man had nothing to do with this case, as many a colored man has been a guest at his house."

The colored citizens who felt indignant over General Smalls's reception at the Revere called a meeting last evening at Bethel Hall on North Anderson street, which, after a consultation of the organizers of the same, was postponed indefinitely.

Uncle Romulus

As my brother, a Nascar fan, sometimes says: I started hearing the sound of lug nuts hitting the asphalt.

Initially, Bobby Large seemed to be unaware that I knew. He came strutting into my office for his usual quick chat on the way to class. I pretended nothing had changed. Meantime, I imagined the purplish enormity swaying inside those ridiculous, baggy pants. I imagined my sweet Grace unzipping, cupping the black Mamba lovingly in her hands and raising...

O.k. I was a grown man. It was the 21st Century. I could handle this maturely. I couldn't help the internal monologue running in my head. I could, at least control what I did and said.

But genes are strong. And the genes I carry, the ones that keep a man from controlling what he says and does, those genes run even stronger in my father and brother, and for the love of God, what might come out of their mouths if this went anywhere?

We're talking about Grace here, so of course it did go somewhere. It went somewhere like the Nascar field running into a high-banked turn at the Charlotte Motor Speedway.

The Yankee Paper

Boston Daily Globe, July 19, 1882, first page, above the fold:

SMALLS VS. TILLMAN

Another Partisan Outrage in the House

An Attempt to Seat a Man who was Never Elected

How the Republicans Hope to Capture Southern Districts

(Special Dispatch to *The Boston Globe*.)

WASHINGTON, July 18- The Republicans in the House began today another of the partisan outrages whereby they hope to be able to capture several Southern congressional districts in the next election. They secured the attendance of a quorum to unseat George D. Tillman, who was elected by 8038 majority in the fifth South Carolina district, and place

Robert Smalls (colored) in Tillman's seat. Smalls claimed 1480 majority on the following assertions:

First, because large numbers of votes were cast for him which were not counted for him by the precinct managers.

Second, because large numbers of votes counted for him by the precinct mangers were unlawfully rejected by the county canvassers.

Third, because from the three counties of Barnwell, Colleton and Edgefield, the returns and poll lists were not forwarded to the Governor and secretary of state as provided for by law.

Fourth, because of violence and intimidation in all the counties composing the fifth congressional district, except Beaufort, whereby, as he claims, many of his adherents were prevented from voting for him.

The evidence taken by the elections committee failed in every respect to sustain those charges. Regarding the first charge, if all the testimony offered on behalf of the contestant be taken as true, it would not materially affect the result of the election, but the testimony was repeatedly impeached by credible witnesses. There is not a word of testimony throughout the entire record tending, however remotely, to prove the truth of the second charge...

Uncle Romulus

In my father's and brother's defense, and I mean this from my heart, they weren't in their right minds after we lost my sister, Grace's mother. It was a terrific blow for all of us.

The years of dysfunction and drug abuse had taught me to detach from my sister. She knew not to come to me with her bullshit by the end of her life. But my dad and brother were caught in her web of co-dependence. They felt they ran her life. Eventually they felt their actions were necessary to sustain the operation of the universe in accordance with their plans. My sister's decision to take her own life was completely out of sync with their plans for the orderly unfolding of time across the universe, and this had upset them greatly.

I, on the other hand, took my sister's suicide as... what? How can you describe surviving a suicide to someone who hasn't had to do it? You can write some bullshit like I wrote above. You can make up all kinds of witty nonsense to say. But maybe all you can truthfully say is that there is a pain like none you ever imagined. Is guilt the right way to name this pain? I've heard that word used a lot in connection with surviving suicide. But I don't think guilt quite gets to what is so painful about it. I think it's the utter loss of hope. The utter failure of grace. It is as if that purported arc of the purportedly moral purported universe didn't bend at all. As if it just shot straight out toward the Andromeda galaxy, toward that fuzzy smudge of light you can see with the naked eye on a crystal clear night, if you know where to look, with no bend, no arc to it at all. It's just headed way out there, too big to understand, too distant, too impossible, too much not giving the slightest goddamn about you. Not the slightest goddamn after all.

Seems selfish. You're talking about someone else's pain here. Someone else's disease and death. But what hurts is you.

If you've never been there, you just don't know. You don't know what it takes to make the man who feeds on grace every minute of every day scream, scream into his pillow.

The truth is none of us was doing too awfully well at the particular moment in our lives, some couple of years after Grace's mom had opened the top of her head with the shotgun, when Bobby Large walked up the brick entry path of my father's house with Grace glowing beside him.

Bobby. Sweet Bobby. He was scared to death. I could tell it by the roll and strut. I knew him well enough to read it. As they reached the front door, Grace snatched the ridiculous, flat-rimmed ball cap from his head. He looked as if she had suddenly disrobed him, right before he was to enter the lion's den.

And believe me, he was about to enter the lion's den. Not that anyone behaved badly that afternoon. I thought my mother, a former Junior League president, had never- never in the fifty years I'd known her- been so gracious, dignified, well-mannered, positive as she was that afternoon.

My father, God help him, behaved better than he had in twenty years. They did everything they could to make Bobby feel at home, to allay their darling Grace's fear. My brother, not as smooth on his best days as his parents, also managed quite well. If you didn't know what was going on beneath the surface you really would think these people thought they were meeting the most promising young couple in town.

Bobby. Poor Bobby. He looked as if he wished the earth would open and swallow. After a while, though, after I had done my very, very best to communicate my continued good will and genuine friendship, I began to see the hope in his eyes. I could see the arc-bending, universe-aligning hope that maybe, just maybe, he could really be welcomed into our world. That he really could do it.

And Grace simply glowed. Poor manic, delusional Grace. Beautiful beyond description. More beautiful than my memory can picture her.

The meeting went supernaturally well. I can't remember it going any better when one of my own daughters brought a boyfriend from real college to meet their grandparents. It was just golden.

I walked with Grace and Bobby to his car afterwards. Grace turned suddenly and hugged me, squeezing me tight with abandon, a hug I can still feel, with a pain and loss that aches to the core of me.

I happened to glance inside Bobby's car as Grace was hugging me. On the console beside the driver's seat lay a nine-millimeter Glock pistol, black as the ace of spades.

Uncle Romulus

To tell Smalls's story, you'd get to this point, sometime in his mid-40's, where, like so many people's story, it sort of becomes something else.

I think Smalls's story, at this point, becomes the story of all of us in middle age. He clings desperately to what he became, the King of Beaufort County, the Captain of the *Planter*, the champion of the colored man. But he is losing. He is being shoved into irrelevance by forces more powerful than he.

He dreams, perhaps of making a comeback, of stringing his bow like Ulysses and slaying the suitors. But only our heroes in our made-up stories get to do that. The rest of us simply begin the painful process of crumbling into old age, losing that which is dear to us. Losing those things we built. Having the deeds of courage and accomplishment become nothing but stories, stories that don't even seem entirely real to us any more. Much of what we know about Smalls we owe to his own stories, and the biographers are left with this conundrum: Whom do we believe? Was Smalls the more righteous of the story tellers? Was he the most righteous? Were the others all so led by their own ambitions that their stories can't be believed at all? Or could we look in those stories for grains of the truth?

We also have Smalls's recorded words in his speeches and letters. I've used those alongside the other stories I made up out of whole cloth. In those lies I told while attempting to tell the truth, I adhered as diligently as I could to proven historical fact, to the extent I could discern it in the conflicting details of the historical record. Dig deeper into any historical story, I've found, and it begins to crumble in the details.

So, primarily out of respect for Smalls, I never made up his words. I only used his own words.

But are those really his words? Clearly, some of the letters I've used were not written by Smalls himself. You can see it in the handwriting. There is the immaculate, disciplined penmanship of the letter, and there is Smalls's scrawled signature at the end, in a hand more believably that of a man who was illiterate until his 20's.

Smalls's daughter Elizabeth, educated at fine New England schools, served as his secretary during most of his political career, so I assume I am reading a letter dictated to her by her father. But to what extent did she edit? To what extent did she correct the grammar? Was he truly that eloquent himself?

There are his speeches in the Congressional Record, where he is so quick on his feet and so bitingly glib in deflating his opponents. But the Congressional Record can be edited by the Congressmen themselves before it is published, so is the speech that is recorded really his speech as it was given?

Now, let's turn to the problem of Smalls in middle age. He's still got a couple of terms in Congress left to go in the story. But I think perhaps the more interesting part, at this point, is to deal with Hannah. I've been reluctant to play the part of any of Smalls's family members. I have felt his family was off limits. Perhaps his descendants, apparently such decent and public-minded American citizens, might be offended. As if they wouldn't be offended by everything else I'm writing here. Oh well.

Hannah. We have photographs. In middle age. The wife of the King of Beaufort County. Several years his senior. Mother of his children. Mother of another man's children. She is pinched looking. She is not pretty. She does not inspire. What should I do with her?

He stayed. We have little to go on here, except family lore that says Smalls's real marriage of love was with Annie, the second wife. So where does that leave Hannah?

Think, now, what Hannah has lived through with Robert. Think of the young slave couple living in an outbuilding in Charleston, negotiating her purchase and the purchase of her children from her owner. What did she think of young Robert (quite the dashing young man, we know from his photographs), and what must he have thought of her?

Was she there as he planned the theft of the *Planter*? Did the conspirators, in fact, meet in her home (as some historians maintain?) Did she, like the others who planned the escape, agree to blow the ship up rather than allow herself to be captured? If so, she was agreeing to kill her own children, her husband's stepchildren, in support of his wild plan to change their lives.

Think when he was off fighting the war, gone for much of the next three years, and she was home, dealing with the death of their first-born son from a childhood illness. The child died around the time of the Folly Creek incident that made Robert captain of the *Planter*.

I've told the story of a man's life here, but have I told the true story? I didn't even tell you that part yet. We went through those years with plenty of action, with plenty of history, with plenty that you would like to read, but here was the part of it that was the real story of his and Hannah's lives. This was the part they would remember. This is the part they would really care about. This is the part they wouldn't really want to talk about for the rest of their lives, because it would be eating at their hearts and digging at the foundations of their faith. And by all accounts, they were the most faithful of people.

We haven't even gone there, really, because how in the world do you go into that secret world of silent prayer that is the real life of people like that? The continuing, day-long dialogue with a God who appears not to be there. They hear the other Voice, the one that answers, that tells them what to do, that may be nothing but a figment of their imagination, but they continue to talk, and to listen, and this conversation goes on and on and becomes the very essence of their life, its full and complete purpose, until all else is merely who loved whom and who hated whom and what the weather was like.

We have some record of this conversation. We can't tell if it's true. I have never told it in this story, because I don't have any confidence that these were Smalls's exact words, actually. All biographers, virtually all historians, record the words of this silent prayer, purportedly spoken (but not really spoken) by Smalls as the *Planter* approached Fort Sumter in that pre-dawn time of horror.

They say he prayed to God to deliver him and his fellow travelers from danger as He delivered the children of Israel from bondage. Something to that effect. I don't know the exact words. Only He knows them, if the conversation was ever held. If it was held, it appears, on the surface at least, the answer was positive.

Of course, the only way anyone would know of this snippet of the ongoing, secret, silent conversation of life, would be if Smalls retold it, which he apparently did, again and again, to anyone who would listen. Who knows if he was telling the truth in these stories? If, as many serious, respectable newspapers reported during his lifetime, he was in fact cowering in the hold of the *Planter* at this moment in history, while one of his other crew members piloted the ship out of the harbor, then the story was not true.

Well, he could have had that conversation no matter where he was standing.

And now, I guess, we might as well get around to the bigger question here. Smalls was asking something awfully big if he was indeed in command of the ship, and if he did indeed ask this as they steamed past Fort Sumter. The prayer was almost immediately granted by the Almighty Himself. (Or was it granted by Smalls himself, you might ask?)

And yet, as we are beginning to see, ultimately it was all taken back. The story of Robert Smalls's life, you see, is the story of a man who led his people out of bondage, only to spend the rest of his life watching them be delivered right back into it.

And so, think back now to the youngish Hannah who sat in those clandestine meetings with her dashing, much younger husband, and imagine the most eventful, and dangerous, and exciting, and fulfilling, and uplifting, and terrifying, and heartbreaking, and tedious, and soul-crushing of lives. In that one, quick feat of imagination, (which is, after all, nothing more than reflecting on our own lives) we can carry ourselves once again to the house on Prince Street in Beaufort. Let's imagine ourselves stepping onto the shaded front porch, and let's enter by the front door. Let's climb the stairway in the entry hall, and let's turn right into the master bedroom. And there, let us watch as Hannah, wife of the King, sickens and dies.

As will we all. It won't be long, really.

Uncle Romulus

Meanwhile, at the other end of existence, Bobby Large and Grace were engaging in the procreative arts, listening no doubt to Hip Hop, twiddling Grace's red-gold hair between their fingers, expressing the essence of humanity.

They were doing the procreative act, wholly and with abandon. They were recombining the African with the European, making little Americans, but their youth and their culture prepared them not one whit for the consequences. Procreation was far from their minds.

Let us question then, the premises of this union.

First, is love involved? Sex without love is possible. It happens. Many of us have experienced it. We can watch it on our televisions. We watch it on our computers. We can watch it on our cell phones.

But if we are honest, is the hope for love not intrinsically contained in the act? Is it not seminal? Is the humping of the young idiot at its root not the act of hope and love, a desperate and ill-guided act, perhaps, but far more about love and hope than it is about glands?

Some biologists will have us believe sex is simply motivated by the drive to perpetuate and distribute our genetic material, as if this were the impetuous force of our existence. But I myself have never felt such an urge. I have, to the contrary, been face to face with the almost irrepressible urge to destroy my genetic material along with myself. You went there with me when we climbed those attic stairs earlier in our story. I question, therefore, whether a desire to perpetuate genes, even at the unconscious level, truly exists in human beings.

The hope and love impetus, if this is truly what is at work here (You must ask yourself the honest question here. You must be still, and listen, in that prayerful conversation you shrink from,) the hope and love impetus does not really care about the perpetuation of genetic material. It cares for itself. It cares for hope and love entirely on their own. It grasps for hope and love in any direction, at times in the most self-destructive of directions, in the most fruitless of directions, in the most hurtful of ways, but in the ways that truly drive our existence and explain the pain and the insanity. Ultimately, hope and love may be the cause of all things human, I fear.

And then you have Grace. I knew Grace. I knew what drove her. I knew that she was nothing except the search for love and the frantic grasping for hope, directed by insanity. And I knew Bobby Large. Bobby was nothing except the search for love and the frantic grasping after hope, steered not by his own insanity, but by the self-destructive insanity of his own culture. Perhaps you think I am talking about the insanity of African-American culture. But I am talking about the insanity of American culture. The African part of that is thrown in for free. It's just a part of our genetic material.

And let us talk about the action of Grace in this entire affair. For Grace is what makes it all happen. And what is Grace, you ask? Grace can be defined as an undeserved gift from God. I suppose a beautiful, genetically insane child would be an undeserved gift. Surely we didn't deserve her. Surely Bobby Large didn't deserve her. And now that she is gone, there is no question, in the silent core of my being, that she was truly a gift. The most precious of gifts.

So, let us roam for a moment in our imaginations through the absurd, drug- and alcohol-fueled early-morning party scene, thrummed by the self-killing Hip Hop rant, peopled by the semi-literate, utterly ignorant, marginally employable youth of our South Carolina town. Let the hope and love that created and sustained Bobby and Grace carry us to this sweating, beautiful, bumbling union of the bodies, the dark with the milky, the strong with the supple, the hoping with the hoping. Let us go there for a moment and ask what was really happening.

Go there for a moment and be silent.

And silent.

And silent.

Uncle Romulus

I've skipped ahead a bit. We've got two more Congressional elections to go. But this part of the story confuses and bores me, to be honest. The politics become so convoluted. The narrative gets so zig-zaggy. It's hard to stay interested.

Before Hannah's death, the South Carolina legislature, controlled by Democrats, had carved out parts of Smalls's Congressional District so as to give George Tillman a safe district farther to the north and west, containing, among other places, Edgefield and Hamburg. So Tillman was out of Smalls's way. Beaufort County was now part of the Seventh Congressional District, predominately African-American and known statewide as the Black District. There would be no Democratic candidate for this seat. Now Smalls's fellow Republicans, the predominately black members of the party he had founded in South Carolina, were standing in his way.

After many, many deadlocked ballots at the district Republican caucus, Smalls withdrew and put his support behind E.M. Mackey, a white candidate, as opposed to the other black candidate, who had campaigned against Smalls by saying Smalls was an agent of the corruption that plagued the Republican party in South Carolina during Reconstruction. Mackey, by the way, was married to a black woman. Mackey won the Republican nomination, passed uncontested through the general election, and soon died. Smalls was appointed to take his place. This was in 1882.

And then Hannah died. And then Smalls ran for Congress again in the 1884, defeating a white Democrat attorney and Confederate veteran, William Elliott.

And, so he was a Congressman for about four more years. Is this really an important part of Robert Smalls's life, or is this just the powerful mid-life distraction that sucks us away from the real business of living? Robert Smalls was a great man, and I don't believe this period is particularly part of his greatness.

Smalls did, however, make one delightful, short speech on the floor of Congress during this time. He was, at the moment, arguing in favor of a bill he had introduced to provide a pension to the widow of General Hunter. You remember Hunter- the General who freed the slaves, if only for a moment, and received young Robert in the tree-frog-ringing woods of Hilton Head after the young slave had stolen the *Planter*. The General who sent Smalls to see

President Lincoln. The General who fed so much hope and love into young Robert.

Congressman Smalls introduced a bill to provide a pension to General Hunter's widow, General Hunter having passed into eternity in roughly the same time frame as Smalls's beloved Hannah. Smalls's bill passed Congress, and President Cleveland later vetoed it. So the bill, ultimately, was pointless. It carried no real historical significance, like most of Smalls's Congressional actions.

But during the debate in Congress, Robert Smalls offered this snippet which should speak to the heart of any American who has ever listened to the stories told of our country, especially since it was delivered by a man who would be completely forgotten by America by the time he died, a man who was blotted from the history books for the better part of a century. The year was 1885:

> Mr. Speaker, by the variations and methods of modern politics, my race of upward seven millions of people are represented on this floor by the honorable gentleman from North Carolina and myself. How long this injustice will be tolerated I will not dare to prophesy; but so long as one of us be permitted on this floor our voice and vote will not be withheld from any measure of legislation which will add to the prosperity and happiness of all the people, without regard to color or condition, and the permanence and greatness of a common country.

The Governor

In 1886, the black cancer was removed from Congressional Office in our state. The most dangerous man in South Carolina was finally recognized, even by his own people, for what he was.

I traveled to Beaufort for a public rally in support of our Democratic candidate, a Confederate veteran and the most upright of men- the kind of man we need in public office, the kind of man we have so diligently worked to restore to leadership in this great state.

As I was speaking, I saw Smalls coming. He walked- rather he waddled, fat as he was- at the head of his band of militia. General Smalls. My Lord, what a farce. The toy general marching his toy black soldiers to meet the real general.

Their uniforms were a disgrace to the United States military. Bright blue cloth. Shiny brass buttons. Shiny brass helmets topped with swaying, white egret plumes. Their faces were black as marsh mud. All you could see was white eyes and teeth. It was an absurd sight. Their brass band played an African beat.

Smalls marched them disrespectfully up to the front of the assembly. It was a brazen action, interrupting a speech by a United States Senator- a former Governor of the State. I held my composure, but I called him out.

I called him out, there in public, in front of his own people, exactly for what he was, a felon, convicted by a jury of his peers, most of them colored men themselves. A bribe-taker. I could see the ire rising in his face as I spoke, but I spoke the truth, and the truth can have that effect.

Then Smalls, the rascal, rose up and called me out in public, accusing me of defrauding the widow in Mississippi. My God! The audacity of that Negro. It only goes to show how radically unfit for public office he was. How utterly unfit for public discourse, unqualified to participate in the public affairs of decent, honorable men. I answered him coolly, curtly, and with disdain.

We defeated him in that election- removed him from elective office for the remainder of his life. That was what broke the Negro hold on our state for good. There were briefly two later Negro congressmen from that district. There was Miller, who called himself a Negro, but looked no blacker than I. And then later that scoundrel Murray who defeated him. Within another ten years, we were done with Murray, and the black era in the history of our state had come to a close.

Uncle Romulus

Accusations of fraud against Governor Wade Hampton were widespread and well-documented. *The New York Times* detailed the accusations in a December 27, 1876 article. In brief- although the article is anything but brief- Hampton was accused of borrowing over one million dollars against real estate and other assets worth $140,000 while attempting to re-establish himself as a large-scale planter in Mississippi after the Civil War.

The list of assets and debts presented to substantiate this charge is, according to the paper, taken from U.S. Court documents filed in Hampton's bankruptcy in Mississippi in 1868. At the time of the publication of the article, Hampton had just been elected governor of South Carolina and was planning the arrest of Congressman Robert Smalls for bribery.

The New York Times alleged Hampton had defrauded his creditors by offering them mortgages on land that had already been mortgaged, without disclosing the previous loans. Near the top of the list of Hampton's creditors was a Mrs. Mary Davis, identified as a widow from Columbia, S.C., who lost ten thousand dollars in the bankruptcy.

The Yankee Paper

Boston Daily Globe, Friday, July 12, 1889, front page, above the fold:

SMALLS ON TOP AGAIN

Once Convicted of Fraud and Bribery,

Now Holding Sway in a Custom House Down South.

Life of the Foxiest of All the Colored Politicians.

NEW YORK, July 11.- The World prints the story of the life of Robert Smalls of South Carolina and some inside facts on the politics of that State. The following is a digest of it:
BEAUFORT, S.C. July 11.- The custom house in Beaufort port stands with its back to the water and its face to the

sleepy main street, which skirts the river front.

There was a moving last week in the old gray building. Democratic Collector Richardson packed up his traps and made ready to go back to his up-country plantation to farm rice and shoot and ride horseback.

Today the new regime holds sway behind the counters in the custom house. Robert Smalls, round, black, and with the white cravat and all the unction of an African Methodist bishop, keeps the keys and gathers the imposts.

Off shore 300 yards away a big revenue cutter, gay in flags, lies anchored where he can have his eye on her, and all up and down the village streets knots of colored Republicans can be overheard at whatever hour of day you will plastering the name Smalls with execration, and alternating it now and then with anathema upon the head of Harrison.

The history of Smalls, so far as it is on the surface, is worth reading. He was born a slave, the property of the McKees, one of the best families in South Carolina. Smalls has brains, and the first marks of that shrewd intelligence which has made him far and away the foxiest politician in South Carolina, showed themselves when, at an early age, he got himself hired out as a waterman about the Charleston docks, his wages, of course, being paid to his owner.

He gained fame in the early days of the war as being the chap who succeeded in running the *Planter* out of Charleston harbor. They say now that he didn't do it at all; that the job was planned and executed by a modest man named Alston, but when they reached the transport Smalls jumped aboard hurriedly, began to wag his tongue, take the credit, vaunt himself and his reputation was made. Alston kept still.

The reconstructionists took great stock in Smalls. They pushed him along, and he knew he was a winning card. In 1865, he was elected to the State Senate from Beaufort county.

The annals of the venality, robbery and all species of abuses during those reconstruction days would give a purist in politics a congestive chill.

In the ascendancy of the "party of moral ideas" Smalls was head and front.

By and by reaction came. There were too many fingers in the pie. The State couldn't stand it. Corruption had reached high water mark.

By 1874 Smalls was convicted on charges of fraud and bribery by a jury composed mostly of colored men and sentenced to two years in the penitentiary. Appeal was taken to the Superior court of the State, and the case was certified to the United States Supreme Court. Before the appeal could be tried influence was set to work, and suddenly Smalls was pardoned by Gov. Simpson.

Then Smalls was free to go his course again. He resumed the function of dictator to the vote in the colored district, and was at the top of the heap. Houses, carriages, horses were his. His aspirations knew no bounds. He never pretended to consult the party organization, but made it consult him.

When Smalls's appointment as collector was hinted at there was sent to Washington a long petition in opposition to it. Word had been sent to Washington that Smalls was getting signers to petitions in favor of himself and would be appointed unless some voice of objection was raised by Beaufort folks, telling what he had done to the people. Objections of every conceivable description were made, but Ben Harrison was for Smalls and that ended it.

Now Smalls rides abroad in state.

Aside from the trifling foibles herein recounted the character and life of Mr. Harrison's appointee are all right, so far as the general public is informed, and he is fit to take office along with Dudley, Wanamaker and the large family of Scotts, Harrisons and McKees.

Uncle Romulus

What the hell does Hispanic mean? It's actually classified as a race in most U.S. Government documents. I am quite sure it is nothing of the sort. I am not at all sure what "Hispanic" means. In the American mind, it means vaguely that you came from Mexico, that, in other words, you are "Spanish." That you come from somewhere "down there." Like Brazil.

It is a ridiculous concept. It has nothing to do with race. Or maybe it has everything to do with race, which is to say that it simply demonstrates the concept of race is a mental hat rack on which we can hang our stupidest ideas and predilections.

But the American concepts of Black and White, surely, do clearly hinge upon real racial characteristics. You have the Sub-Saharan African. You have the white-skinned European. Well, think about that for a moment. In your mind, take a little imaginative journey with me.

Let's start at the shores of the Arctic, and then let's look at folk, just regular folk, from Lapland (They're not Eskimos, are they? They're white people, right?) Down through Sweden (Leggy blonds? That's white people.) Across to Holland (Stubbier blonds?) Swing south to France (Brunette white people.) Cross the Pyrenees to Spain, where (once you get beyond the Basque country) you will spend some time with real Spanish people (they don't really LOOK Hispanic.) Then you will cross over to Morocco, origin of Othello, the Moor of Venice, played by lily-white Orson Welles in pancake makeup, or by jet-black descendants of Sub-Saharan Africans, but rarely by anyone who looks like an actual Moor. And then travel south across the Sahara, among the Bedouin and Tuareg, to mysterious Timbuktu, where Arab meets Negro (sometimes with violence), and then down the Niger river to the homeland of the Igbo people themselves.

You can see, perhaps, in this journey through the mind's eye, that the concept of race is about as clear cut as the concept of good and evil. If we want to draw a line, it's going to take a lot of self-deception. But people so want to draw those lines. The world is so much easier if there is black and white. If there is good and evil. If there is Hispanic. If there is Jew and goyim. If there is racist and whatever the opposite of that is. If there is moral and immoral.

So, when Robert Smalls and Pitchfork Ben Tillman set to defining the line between black and white in South Carolina, they, two masterful politicians that they were, were playing a tune that would get a whole state dancing. It was a beat that was bound to get feet tapping everywhere. Hips would start to sway. Smiles would start to form. Arms would lift in joy, and everyone would start to move in unison, to go with the dance their genes made them want to dance... but I'm getting way ahead of myself here.

The Great, Great

So when Ben Tillman got me appointed postmaster in Newberry, South Carolina, I've got to admit it was a stroke of grace. As I've said, I never really thought much of the man. I had a poor opinion of him since I came home from the war and heard he sat it out for losing his eye. But Tillman was a politician, and I've got to admit, he had a spot in his heart for the common man. He always seemed to remember me as someone who supported him when the Red Shirts were starting up.

When my business failed, it was the darkest time of my life. When Tillman came up with the postmaster idea, I jumped at it. It did save me. It saved my family. It saved me from ruin and bankruptcy, and I've got to be grateful to the man. I certainly wasn't the only former Confederate officer to face bankruptcy in my lifetime. Look at Governor Hampton's troubles, for goodness sake.

These have been hard times we've lived through. Ben Tillman finally gave me a way to live through them.

It got me involved with the postal service, and that was worthwhile. I got involved eventually in the fight to oppose the civil service system. There were those who had been working, especially since the assassination of President Garfield, to end patronage in government jobs. Well, patronage was how I got my job. It was how we all got our government jobs. It had worked pretty darn well since the time this country was founded. It kept government employees accountable to the people, and those who wanted to change the system just wanted to hold on to their fat government jobs after the politician who appointed them had lost his.

At any rate, I got involved in the national movement to oppose the civil service, and Governor Tillman encouraged me to get more involved. That was how I found myself on a train from Columbia to Washington, D.C., and how I ended up sitting next to Congressman Miller.

I sat down beside what I took to be a white man, one I had never seen before. He was as white as I am. I learned pretty quickly that he was just about exactly as white as I am.

We got to talking, and I told why I was going to Washington and asked why he was, and he let on he was a Congressman. I was interested, and I asked more. Although he was shy at first, and I kind of had to pull it all out of him, in the end, I realized he was the Congressman from the Black District, the one Robert Smalls used to represent. And I said, fool that I was, that it was a wonderful thing that we had finally gotten that seat out of the hands of the niggers.

Miller didn't get angry. He turned red in the face, but he didn't lose his temper, and he quietly and politely informed me that he was, in fact, a colored man himself.

I was dumbfounded. I didn't know what to do. He didn't look any more colored than I do. Which, it turns out, he wasn't. But I realized other people in the car might have recognized the man. There I was on my first official trip to Washington on government business, and I was sitting in the seat right next to a colored man.

I collected myself and remembered my upbringing. I struck up a conversation with Miller, just as friendly and polite as I could. As the next couple of hours went on, out came pretty near his whole life story.

His mother had been colored, a high yellow gal out of Charleston, whose father was a signer of the Declaration of Independence. And Miller's father had been the white son of prominent planters from the Low Country. Miller's father had been in love with the high yellow gal, who was just about white to anybody who would look at her, but his family, as high-born as they considered themselves, would have nothing of it, and they threatened to disown him if he married her.

So the high yellow gal had the Congressman as a bastard, yellow child and gave him up for adoption. A real colored family adopted and raised him. By raising, and partially by blood, he was a real colored man.

He told his story just as straightforward as any man might talk about his family. It became obvious to me the only difference between him and me was I was raised in a white family. It made my grandmother's story easier for me to understand, maybe, since I had never been told the story, and I didn't understand how the colored blood got mixed in our family, exactly. Nobody ever talked of it at all. Maybe my grandmother had fallen for one of these high yellow types herself. I mean, my father didn't look any more colored than this Congressman Miller did.

It was a big moment in my life, really. I realized just how blessed by the Almighty I was. My grandmother had taken the pains to move to a new town and make her son white, and keep our family name clear. Because I could have ended up just like this nigger, for goodness' sake.

I almost forgot the shame of sitting next to a colored man on a public train.

After lunch, Congressman Miller began to nod in his seat. Quick as he fell asleep, I quietly got up and moved to a seat in another car, farther toward the rear of the train, where he was less likely to find me if he got up to walk around.

Uncle Romulus

We've got two love stories brewing, now. We've got Grace and Bobby Large, and we've got Robert Smalls and Annie Wiggs. Smalls, that aging has-been, now the customs inspector in Beaufort, meets the much younger, beautiful school teacher, and, by all reports, falls madly in love.

Grace, the young never-will-be, meets Robert Lewson, thug of hope, dreamer of dreams, and finds that for which she had been searching her whole life

Lewson... I remember when I first saw the name on my class roster. I glanced up, surprised at that rarest of things, a Jewish student at a community college in South Carolina. The man who would be Bobby Large answered the call.

Lewson... I broached the subject once when I met his mother, wondering where the name had come from. She said it was Robert's father's name, and he was not involved in Bobby's life. I had gleaned from Bobby in class discussion that his father was white, although Bobby himself looked no more white than Robert Smalls does in photographs.

So, Bobby Large, the young Jew, is my niece's vessel of hope. And Annie Wiggs, young Negress, is the hope of General Smalls, that increasingly rotund, increasingly gray, increasingly irrelevant, former King of Beaufort County. Smalls's children and Hannah's are grown now, educated in fine schools, already beginning to flee South Carolina as the campaign of ethnic cleansing gathers momentum, moving on to other parts of the country.

Meanwhile, Robert Smalls, the man who refuses to live in despair, falls in love with young Annie, marries her in a ceremony attended by his still-numerous admirers and friends, black and white. And he fathers the son of his old age, Willie.

They live in the Prince Street house.

Grace and young Lewson move into his mother's apartment. They spawn a son themselves. The quarter-Jew. The quarter-Negro (forgetting the minuscule traces of the Negro in Grace's lineage, and the substantial possibility of further European admixture in Bobby's).

Smalls, it seems, faired a bit better in this exercise. We have no historical record of the hormone-fueled pregnancy of Annie, a woman who would have been in her late thirties at the time of this pregnancy. But I am about to render into written history the effect of pregnancy hormones on a twenty-year-old young woman suffering from Borderline Personality Disorder, and it is not pretty.

It's so much easier and neater, it makes so much more believable a story, if I put clinical, scientific names on it, doesn't it? Let's look at it as a young child would, as young Grace did, when as a red-headed toddler, she witnessed the drug-fueled insanity of her mother and the various live-in men, rampaging through the rental houses and apartments they inhabited. Imagine, from the height of about two-and-a-half feet, the screaming, the tears, the violence, the retching, the words meant to tear apart and disembowel and destroy forever. Let's be that little, wide-eyed, red-haired girl, hiding behind the couch, clutching at her stuffed, purple dinosaur. Hoping that Uncle Rom would come. Hoping he would take her to his house. Try to put a name on this. Try to put a diagnosis on it. Maybe you would just be reasonable about it and conclude that hope is a useless fantasy, bearing no relation to reality at all.

On the other hand, we could imagine ourselves as young Willy. His father is the stately, portly General Smalls. Always immaculately attired. His house is large. His father adores his mother. He treats her as a queen. He comports himself as a King, he treats his wife as the vessel of grace, and he dotes on young Willy as, almost half a century earlier, planter Henry McKee doted on his young slave Robert in the same house. Willy would need no diagnosis, no clinical names to make his story make sense. Hope and grace and love would be the foundation of the universe. Pitchfork Ben Tillman, the one-eyed architect of genocide, America's proud advocate of the Master Race, would be nothing more than an aberration, an irrelevancy to be ignored, data to be fudged and manipulated away, because it does not work with the sensible hypothesis.

I feel for Bobby Large. I have always felt for him. He brought the beautiful, eloquent, intensely loving Grace into his bed and home, and he loved her, and he brought forth the promise of life in her womb, and she became something more terrifying than Pitchfork Ben Tillman himself.

Uncle Romulus

A Polish-Jewish Holocaust survivor named Raphael Lemkin wrote the definition of genocide in the Geneva Convention. He invented the word. Before Lemkin, there was no name for genocide, and there was no law banning it.

My charge that the government of South Carolina, with the complicity of the United States Government, engaged in genocide against African-Americans during the Jim Crow era certainly demands examination.

First, we should examine arguments that clear the American conscience of the crime of genocide.

These arguments have been made before, in public, in an op-ed in *The New York Times*, by none other than Raphael Lemkin himself. In 1951, an organization of American Negroes calling itself the Civil Rights Congress filed a complaint with the United Nations entitled *We Charge Genocide.* The report accused the United States Government of genocide against Negroes. The complaint was delivered to the U. N. in New York by internationally famous singer Paul Robeson, among others.

Civil rights leader W. E. B. DuBois also planned to deliver the document to U. N. officials in Paris, but the United States government, learning of his intentions, declared him an unregistered foreign agent and prevented him from traveling to France.

The document was ignored by the mainstream press in the United States.

Some black newspapers in the U.S. reported on it. The document, however, was widely covered by the international press and made a substantial public impression in other countries. The international Communist movement trumpeted the report (which contained over 200 pages of carefully-documented, largely-undisputed evidence in support of the charge.)

We Charge Genocide only covers events and actions after 1945, the period after the United Nations outlawed genocide.

The charges never went anywhere. The United States government had overwhelming influence in the United Nations at the time. The Civil Rights Congress's connections with international Communism ultimately doomed their appeal and soon led to their dissolution as an organization in the United States.

Lemkin, on the other hand, found the charges disturbing enough that he published an op-ed piece in *The New York Times* disputing them. A law professor, he made the following arguments against the Negroes' charges: 1) they were distracting attention from real genocide that was taking place in the Soviet Union. 2) genocide required the intent to destroy a people, which was clearly not the case in the United States, since the Negro population was actually growing.

I'm no lawyer. I know the law often works in ways the logical mind doesn't, but I can't really follow Lemkin's arguments. His first argument seems to be, essentially: genocide only takes place against, white, Jewish people, so shut up. His argument is much more eloquent. It is more measured, and it sounds more responsible. But I don't think I have substantially mischaracterized it.

If Lemkin really meant his second argument when he drafted the law, why does the law say genocide requires "the intent, in whole *or in part*, to destroy?" The intent in the genocide of the American Negro was the intent to destroy in part.

In fairness, while the African-American percentage of the population in South Carolina declined precipitously in the period from 1890 to 1930, absolute numbers of African-Americans in the state increased during that time period. If one of the requirements for genocide is that you kill people faster than new ones can be born, then what happened during the Jim Crow era was not genocide. But that concept is clearly NOT written into the law. It is a concept added by Lemkin afterwards in his *New York Times* op-ed trying to make sure colored folk didn't take over his idea.

In the decades since he drafted his law, we have seen genocide happen around the world, time and again, against all kinds of people, of all colors. So in our 21st-Century minds the concept more easily applies to black victims. Take, for example what Arabs in the Sudan did to the Negro population of Darfur in recent years. They employed a campaign of violence and terror to drive the Negroes out of their country. The International Criminal Court has indicted the President of Sudan for genocide. With that as recent precedent, it is easier for me to look at what Ben Tillman and my great, great grandfather were doing in the first half of the 20th Century and call it genocide.

In 1992, the United Nations Security Council established the concept of ethnic cleansing as a crime against humanity that could be prosecuted in the International Criminal Court. Their action was in response to Serbian violence against Muslims in Bosnia. The Security Council asserted that while ethnic cleansing itself had not yet been specifically addressed by international law, the actions involved in ethnic cleansing clearly could be prosecuted as violations of the law banning genocide, which had been established for nearly four decades by that time. They pointed to that law's definition of genocide as "the intent to destroy, in whole *or in part*, ..."

Shockingly, *We Charge Genocide* clearly demonstrates the campaign of terror against American Negroes in the South was still going on after the Second World War, in my parents' and grandparents' lifetime, when Eleanor Roosevelt was the U.S. Ambassador to the United Nations. But I already knew that. Most

Americans of a certain age know it. They just don't want to think about it too much.

Lemkin's argument also points out something quite interesting about human beings and language. Genocide is an invented word. It caught on quickly as a loaded word, a moniker of absolute evil. To commit genocide is to commit the most heinous, despicable of acts. So, in general, only other people can commit genocide. We can't commit it. It's a rare country where the public admits their own guilt in genocide forthrightly, openly, and often, no matter how glaringly obvious that guilt might be.

It's sort of like racism. Show me someone in the United States who admits he or she is a racist. Only other people can be racists. We don't call ourselves racists.

This brings me to another disturbing conclusion about genocide. Genocide is not committed by governments, I would argue. It is not a case of a few bad people getting into positions of authority and launching a campaign to destroy or drive out people who are different. Genocide requires the willing, hate-fueled participation of the population. It requires leaders who merely tap into and unleash the secret beliefs and desires of a people. To have Jim Crow, you have to have a populace that wants it in their hearts, and you simply need a Ben Tillman to bring out the worst in them.

If you still think Jim Crow doesn't rise to the level of genocide, or even of ethnic cleansing, read Richard Wright's first-hand accounts of a black man living in the Jim Crow South. Or read the novels of William Faulkner.

Jim Crow was a black-face character in a popular, early-1800's American musical. To call what happened in the American South in the eight or nine decades after Reconstruction "Jim Crow" is roughly equivalent to calling the Holocaust "the Shylock era." To refer to this as the "segregation era" is like calling the Holocaust "the time of economic discrimination." Yet these are the terms applied by American historians to our decades of institutionalized racial terror.

Historians have started referring to the era from the late 1870's until the 1890's as the "Redemption" era. That is an old term, dating back to the time of Hampton and Tillman, who viewed themselves as the redeemers of the South. Like "holocaust", it has interesting religious depths of meaning to it. But could we not come up with a religious term that is more appropriate? Say, perhaps, "the Scourging?" "The Via Dolorosa?" How about "the Passion?" That's a nice word to describe those decades when America expiated its sins by torturing, starving, beating, and lynching its Negroes in plain sight of God and the world.

It seems to me lynching is key to a charge of genocide, since it meets the requirements of Part A of Article II of the definition of genocide: "killing members of the group".

If you're Ben Tillman and his successors in South Carolina, and you kill tens or hundreds of thousands of African Americans through denial of food, medical care, sanitation, education, and economic opportunity, do you commit genocide?

What if you're Tillman and his ilk, and you terrorize the population by lynching?

The Tuskeegee Institute is largely credited with compiling the most credible records of lynchings in the United States. According to the Tuskegee Institute, from 1882 to 1968, one hundred fifty-six African Americans were lynched in South Carolina.

Just this past week, I heard a first-hand account of a lynching near Columbia, South Carolina, from a man at my church. When he was a child in the early 1950's, staying at his grandfather's farm, this man saw a line of automobiles driving past the house for about half an hour.

His grandfather told him to stay away from the windows.

The child learned later that a Negro man had been accused of raping a white woman nearby. The crowd of people driving past in cars had captured the Negro suspect. They took the man to a field out in the countryside. They tied ropes to the Negro's arms and legs. They then teamed up to pull the ropes in four directions, ripping the Negro's body apart while he was still alive.

On October 16, 1901, President Theodore Roosevelt invited the founder of the Tuskegee Institute, George Washington Carver to dine with him at the White House. (Carver was Robert Smalls's close friend and regular correspondent) The dinner was nationally reported.

In response, U.S. Senator Ben Tillman publicly condemned the President for dining with a Negro.

"The action of President Roosevelt in entertaining that nigger," Tillman said, "will necessitate our killing a thousand niggers in the South before they will learn their place again."

Apparently, Tillman accomplished his goal without having to kill quite that many, at least in South Carolina.

Or maybe he meant killing them by starvation.

Uncle Romulus

So- Robert Smalls is the increasingly gray-haired, increasingly portly customs collector in sleepy Beaufort, South Carolina. He is married to the much younger Annie. He is the doting father of little Willie. His other children are well-educated, thriving members of the African-American middle class, coping, as is he, with the waxing climate of oppression and terror against their kind in the American South and in other parts of the country as well.

And, in our parallel sequence of events slightly more than a century later, Bobby Large is living with my pregnant, insane niece in that part of town where she is the only recognizably white person by the time everybody finally goes to bed at night. Her lover's mother, formidable presence that she is, is dealing with the agony of raising young, perpetually misguided Bobby, wrestling with the memory of the dashing Jew who impregnated her and left her twenty years earlier in New York City, ending whatever hopes and dreams she had then and relegating her to single parenthood in the benighted Southern backwater of her youth.

You have Grace's family, my family, ignorant of our own true blackness, knotted in anguish and guilt over Grace's mother's suicide, largely unwilling to accept the diagnoses of Grace's mental illness, understandably confused by the array of diagnoses given to us over the years by different health care professionals. Grace was Grace. She was erratic. She was more erratic than most of us, perhaps, but only in degree, not in pattern. Grace at her worst was just like the rest of us at our worst, but more so. Grace at her best was like the rest of us at our best. But more so.

And now Grace was at her worst and her best. She was in the early stages of pregnancy, aware of her condition, sick in the morning, raging or mooning the rest of the day, skipping her classes at the community college, driving around town in the car my parents had bought her, still smoking despite her pregnancy. I shudder to think what else she was up to.

Poor Bobby. He showed up in my office doorway one morning. He took his hat off. Bobby didn't look silly this morning. He looked real.

I tried to be positive.

"What's up?" I asked.

"Oh, you know. It's all good. It's all good."

A long pause.

"How are your classes going?"

"It's all good. It's all good."

A silence. A rather long one.

"Come on in. You got time to visit?"

He shrugged. He looked up and down the hallway. He hitched his pants up to his waist, came in, and slid into one of the visitor chairs in my office.

"What you up to, Mr. E.?"

"Eh," I searched. "My students think I'm crazy."

He chuckled a little bit. "You like that. That what you love, ain't it?"

"Eh."

Another silence.

"How are things at home?" I asked. I don't know where I found the courage to ask this question.

Bobby's wiggled nervously in his seat. "Oh man."

"Tense?" I said.

"Shit."

We both laughed. We looked at each other and laughed.

"Bobby, you know a pregnant woman can be crazy. I mean..." I waved my hands in front of me.

He reflected for a while.

"Mr. E., I ain't got no daddy. I mean, he ain't never been around. I don't wanna be like that. I don't want my baby to grow up like that."

I wanted to get up and put my arms around Bobby Large and hug him. I wanted to hug him and stroke his head. But I didn't. I didn't.

I told him, as obliquely as I could, how difficult it had been for me as a young man living with a pregnant woman, some twenty-five years earlier.

You can't really tell a young man. I guess he's just got to live through it. And Lord only knows what the young woman does with that memory. My wife, my closest friend and confidant in this life, has never discussed it with me in any honest way. Maybe it's just better to forget it than talk about it. Talking about it isn't going to make it go away. It's going to keep on happening, generation after generation, and after it's over, there will be new babies, and there will be post-partum depression, and there will be fighting and financial worries and heartbreak and joy and love and tears and the most wonderful of times and, in the best moments, in the right moments, we will find the thing that makes us feel the reason for living, and in the worst, we'll find the opposite.

I couldn't explain that to Bobby. We talked about nothing, and it covered everything. At the end of the conversation, when he stood up and moved to the doorway, I followed him and grabbed his hand and shook it.

Then I hugged him, a good man-hug. He tensed when I hugged him. His upper arms held my arms away from his body.

When he left my office, I could see tears in his eyes.

Uncle Romulus

From my readings on Buddhism, I have learned that time may simply not exist. Time may be nothing more nor less than a scaffolding on which we hang our thoughts and perceptions, a concoction of our imagination.

I grasp the stories in this book, I hang them on a hook of time where they seem best to fit. I doubt the people who lived the story would have been able to hang the incidents so neatly on those hooks. I imagine it would all blur together and dance in a sort of vibrating memory dance, like electrons dancing about the atomic nucleus in a quantum-mechanical sort of cosmic hum. There would be no real time to it all, just our desire to make some other sort of order out of it.

I don't think we can necessarily make order out of it. We are searching for an arc running through it, an arc reaching across time, but if time doesn't really exist, and there is no real difference between past and present and future, then the arc itself, needing some sort of dimension in which to exist, could not exist, except perhaps in some quantum-mechanical sort way.

Without time, there would be only one point, and non-point. One vastness and infinity of universalness, one constancy and one unchangingness, one immutability and one mutative constancy of perpetual and instantaneous change. All would be one, and one would be all. The father would be the son, and the son would be the father. The large would be small and the small would be large. The quick would be dead and the dead would be quick. The narrator would be the story and the story would be the narrator. When I told the story, I would be each and every character. When each and every character told the story, they would be each and every me.

If there were no such thing as time, the slave would change into bird and fly away to Africa as easily as the man would change into slave and be delivered unto Georgia, and the slave would sail to freedom as easily as the slavery would creep back into his world. And he would be bold and handsome and young and old and fat and defeated and he would be one, begotten, not made, one in being with the Father, God from God, light from light, true God from True God.

Any arcs that could be drawn, could be drawn only by the grace of God.

There would be the dancing of Shiva, dancing the purported universe into purported being and out of purported being into purported nothingness. Shiva would dance, not as the dervish, whirling about the center, but as the Lord of the Universe, simply doing the Lord's dance, where the slave is free and is bird and is slave and is alive and is dead and is afloat and is drowned and is aloft.

These things would happen, as surely as they happened, as surely as Robert Smalls, King of Beaufort County, Captain of the *Planter*, child of God, chief dancer of the Allen Street Band, and elderly, fat, gray-haired, irrelevant Collector of the Customs in the Port of Beaufort, would be plucked from his growing obscurity by none other than Pitchfork Ben Tillman. Tillman would invite Smalls as one of five Negroes to attend the 1895 Constitutional Convention in Columbia, South Carolina.

Tillman had by this time defeated Wade Hampton finally and absolutely, taking Hampton's U.S. Senate seat, and rendering him into irrelevance. Tillman successfully made Hampton a symbol of wealthy, high-bred, hereditary Southern aristocracy in the coming age of the common man. Tillman would fashion and market himself as the champion of the common man (the white one), and as sure as time, Hampton's day passed for eternity.

This is an interesting development, since Tillman himself was no more a common man or a dirt farmer than Hampton. Tillman was born, raised, and sustained throughout his lifetime in idle, uninterrupted, inherited rural wealth. On the other hand, the white farmer in South Carolina was anything but the common man at that time. He was a member of a decidedly disadvantaged minority in the state.

But Tillman declared the common white farmer to be the common man. And he declared himself to be the apotheosis and champion of such humanity, and having declared his imaginary reality, he set about to make it real, and for that bit of magic, he needed Robert Smalls and a small number of his kind.

Their task, and the task of the attendees at a multitude of state constitutional conventions called across the American South in and around that year, was to make the black man utterly irrelevant- to encode in constitutional law the system of ethnic cleansing that would make that black man ultimately the minority he would become.

Could Ben Tillman foresee Bobby Large? Or was Bobby simply a time future contained in Robert Smalls's time past and Ben Tillman's time present?

Uncle Romulus

In September of 2013, I witnessed the unreality of time first hand. I drove to Savannah, Georgia, and watched Buddhist monks from Drepung Losung monastery in the Himalayas paint a sand mandala.

These Tibetans-in-exile were touring the U.S., performing the entire ritual of sand painting in a new town every week. I watched them at the Savannah College of Art and Design.

In the small exhibition hall where the mandala was taking shape, a Tibetan, throat-singing chant played persistently on loudspeakers. The monks, young-looking men in red robes, were eminently mindful in their artistry. Unmindful Americans huddled around the artists as they worked. A rope line held the unmindful a couple of feet back.

The monks scratched bronze wands across serrations on their silver sand funnels, keeping the rhythm of crickets,. The resulting vibrations lay spidery lines of sand on the painting. The artists followed fine patterns cut into a base layer of green sand.

Occasionally, one monk would stop and cut more patterns into the green base sand, working freehand with a silver scalpel. Sometimes he pulled out a clear acrylic ruler and a schoolboy's metal compass to construct a geometric pattern. Then he went back to the ancient, silver tool to finish the design.

The emerging mandala was symmetrical and organic, perfectly imperfect, perfectly growing and perfectly incomplete. It grew in complexity as I watched them work. I watched, and I watched. I listened, and I listened. I focused. I lost time.

There at the center, in calm repose at the center of the mandala, was a figure. I could not make it out. Was it the Buddha? Was it a god? I stared at the figure in the center of the mandala, trying to see, but I lost myself. The bronze wands scratched the cadence of crickets. The sand flowed into the complexity of the mandala.

Scratch scratch scratch scratch. Scratch scratch scratch.

After some time, which was not time, as far as I know, I looked up from the center. On a long table, just twenty feet or so beyond the mandala, was a framed, color photograph of the 47th Dalai Lama. You know the photo. You've seen it many times. I had seen it when I walked in.

But now I saw it, looking up from the center, and it looked like Robert Smalls. I don't know why. It was not so much the facial features. It was the expression. There was something in the expression I had never seen before, and I can't explain it.

I was in Savannah to help my buddy Tom deliver a boat he had bought, a 42-foot Pearson ketch. Tom had bought the boat on St. Simon's Island and was trying to get it home to North Carolina. The heat exchanger on his Perkins diesel had blown, mid-delivery. Tom had the boat tied up on River Street in historic, downtown Savannah. He was waiting for a new part to be delivered and for a new crew (me) to join him.

I didn't tell Tom I had stopped by the Buddhist sand painting exhibition.

I worked with Tom through that evening, through the next day, and into the following morning replacing the heat exchanger. We had a lot of trouble with it, but we persevered and got the engine running on the third day.

Around lunchtime, we were sitting in the cockpit, eating sandwiches and having celebratory beers. The resurrected diesel purred and belched water beneath us.

Gradually, I became aware of an unusual cacophony of horns and bells approaching.

A steep alley led down to the waterfront from tree-filled Emmet Park on the bluff above. Through the alley came a procession led by the Tibetan monks. They wore their red robes and golden, scrolled helmets. They marched to the riverside, chanting, blowing trumpets, and ringing hand bells. A joyous crowd of Americans followed.

The monks had swept away their sand painting that morning. As I watched, the monks gathered at the river bank. One of the monks said elaborate, incomprehensible prayers.

He poured the brightly colored sand from the mandala into the muddy Savannah River, right off the River Street quay.

At that moment, I realized I must be sitting very near the place where the slaves of Ebo landing were loaded aboard a schooner to sail to St. Simon's.

River Street is not long. The historic waterfront of Savannah has not changed much architecturally in all that time. It must have taken place right there. Right where I was. In another time.

But what if time doesn't exist?

The Statesman

Ben Tillman was the greatest South Carolinian who ever lived, bar none, and you can quote me on that. He took the common man, the ordinary white farmer of South Carolina, the redneck, if you will, and made him King.

And there is everything in the world to be said for that. Because what is the 20th Century but the century of the common man, of real people holding the reins of political power, not just in the United States but eventually the world over?

When I was a young man at the Constitutional Convention in 1895, who would ever have imagined the entire world at war at one time, and the United States at the lead of it all? But it all happened. It happened in my lifetime, and it couldn't have happened without Ben Tillman himself.

He was the founder of Clemson College, you know, where many a young man has gotten the kind of education that would allow him to serve in our armed forces and contribute to the agriculture and engineering of this great country of ours. Strom Thurmond attended Clemson College. Now there are those who would say Thurmond might rise to be the most outstanding South Carolinian who ever lived, now that he's running for president. But Thurmond doesn't rise as high in my estimation as Ben Tillman, who turned this state around and in many ways turned this nation around when he served in the U.S. Senate.

It's the common man in the United States who has proven his mettle in two World Wars, who has defeated the racist Nazi, who has put an end to the horrors and extermination perpetrated by the devilish Jap, and who is restoring a sense of order and decency to the world. The common man is the soul of a nation. The common man carries with him an innate sense of justice and decency. And justice and decency will, we have seen, triumph in the end, no matter how grim things may seem for a while.

Now you ask me about the nigger Smalls. I remember him. Now that you mention him, I do clearly remember him. You have never met a craftier, more devious rascal in your life. They said he was half Jewish, that his former owner was a Jew down in the low country that had sired him on a serving wench in his kitchen. Smalls was convicted of bribery, you know. As I recall, the jury that convicted him was mostly colored men, his own kind, so you can get an idea of the type we're talking about.

We're off the record with all this, right? I mean, if we're just talking straight, I'll be glad to share with you what I remember. Ben Tillman arranged the Constitutional Convention to get the government of the state back in the hands of the white people and put an end to the horrors of reconstruction. Tillman was a master politician. He did everything for a calculated reason. He was always being quoted in the national papers for saying something outrageous, which was why he was called Pitchfork Ben, by the way. But it was all carefully calculated. He never did or said anything unless he'd planned out his strategy like a master chess player.

When we showed up at that convention for the express purpose of getting the colored man out of politics in South Carolina forever, there were half a dozen colored delegates, dressed up in their finest suits, top hats and canes. They arrived riding in their fine carriages. This was the hoi polloi of colored South Carolina, I tell you. Back then you had colored like that. It wasn't like it is now. You still had rich coloreds and high yellows running around living like any white man.

Anyway, here were these five or six nigras, and I couldn't figure out until the whole convention was over exactly what role Tillman had them there to play. They didn't seem to have gotten the message at all. They took off from the beginning like they were there to do something, and it was mighty entertaining to watch for a while.

Now this is off the record, isn't it? You're just using this as background for your story, and none of this is ever, you clear on that boy, EVER going to come back around to me. But that rascal

Robert Smalls, he got in there and turned that convention upside down for a while, and he even got the better of the great and powerful Ben Tillman for a moment.

They parked Smalls off in some irrelevant committee until Tillman could deal him his masterstroke in the end. But Smalls came out of nowhere with something that set the whole thing spinning out of control.

Smalls proposed an article that said no person who cohabited with a negro or mulatto could hold public office anywhere in the state. It was brilliant. I have the most delightful memory of this crafty, old, thieving rascal proposing an article to the Constitution that was exactly the kind of thing Ben had been preaching all along.

The devil in me relishes it. There was Ben Tillman, down at the front of the assembly, a bit surprised by Smalls's proposal, but pleased with it nonetheless, and no doubt contemplating how it should be a part of the Constitution, when Ben's brother George stood up and walked over to Ben. George was as ashen white as if he had just heard of a death in the family.

George grabbed Ben by his coat sleeve and pulled his brother's ear to his mouth and started whispering urgently. Ben got ashen white himself.

And then another delegate walked over as if to join in the conversation, and George turned to that man and said, "Do you mind, sir? Do you mind?"

That man backed away on his heels, and George and Ben started a heated, whispered conversation doing their best not to be noticed. I don't know that anybody but Smalls and me were really paying attention to that little drama. There were a hundred little dramas and conversations going on among all the people in the room, but I was watching the Tillman brothers work themselves into a frenzy. Across the floor that fat, old nigra rascal was just a-beaming in delight.

The convention started getting into the God-awfullest hoo-haw and proposing of wording and amendments that was a sight to behold. What Smalls unleashed is something nobody particularly wanted to talk about.

You had white men having their fun with colored girls all over the state, of course. And of course they wanted that to continue. So they wanted to change the language to disqualify a politician who was married to a colored girl. But Smalls stood up and said that was just the point, really, marriage wasn't the problem, cohabitation was the problem. He said if there were a prohibition against cohabitation with colored women, there wouldn't be enough delegates left in that convention to hold a quorum.

In fact, to pile it on, Smalls proposed wording to require the child of the cohabitation be given the last name of the white father.

Well, you can imagine how that went over. But the subject had been raised, so now Ben Tillman needed to find a way back out of it. He proposed wording to make it illegal to marry a colored girl, or the other way around if you can imagine that ever happening, and saying that anybody with one-eighth colored blood was to be considered colored.

And then his own brother George got up and spoke against Ben's wording, saying there were respectable families from other parts of the state, and he named several counties specifically that would be affected by this definition, that there were respectable families that would be banned from politics if this wording passed. He went on to say there probably wasn't a white delegate in the whole convention that didn't have a drop of some other kind of blood in him somewhere.

Well, when he said that, it had gone far enough. You could have heard a pin drop. As far as I was concerned, he could speak for his damn self.

We didn't get the matter settled that day, and when I walked out of the convention that afternoon, I saw old Smalls standing on the grassy lawn, talking to the other colored delegates. That old rascal wheeled around and jumped up and danced a little jig. Yes, he did.

Marshall Evans

A Musical Interlude

Come, listen all you gals and boys, Ise just from Tuckyhoe;
I'm goin to sing a little song, My name's Jim Crow.
Weel about and turn about and do jis so,
Eb'ry time I weel about I jump Jim Crow

- Lyrics of the song "Jim Crow" popularized by black-faced comedian T.D. "Daddy" Rice in the 1820's and 1830's. This song is said to have given name to the social system established by Ben Tillman and others across the South in the 1890's. Some historians now maintain the song and the character Jim Crow are actually of African origin. Jim Crow, they say, was a bird in African folk tales who avoided trouble by feigning ignorance, deceiving his oppressors, then jumping up and flying away.

Uncle Romulus

Legal scholar Michelle Alexander recently published a book entitled *The New Jim Crow,* in which she says mass incarceration of African-American men in the early 21st Century amounts to a reestablishment of the Jim Crow system in this country. More African-American males are currently held in the American penal system, she points out, than were held in bondage as slaves during the entire two centuries before the Civil War.

I know about the over-incarceration of young black men. In my work in the Governor's office, I toured a number of prisons and jails. Nearly everyone in those places, it seemed, was a young, black man. It was the reverse of walking through fraternity row at my old college, where everyone was a young, white man.

A few years later, teaching in a community college, I'd been exposed to the same reality. Black men in their mid-twenties would show up in my classes wanting to remake their lives after prison, wanting to graduate from college and provide for their illegitimate children. I worked with so many of them. I tried so hard. I seldom succeeded.

Back to Bobby and Grace. I never got a call. They never got me involved at all. I just heard it from one of my daughters. Bobby and Grace had been at a party that got raided by the cops.

The charges did not include possession of the illegal firearm. I don't know where Bobby's gun was when the cops came, but that was not an issue. The issue was possession of crack cocaine. The lovebirds found themselves in jail in the early morning hours, and Grace called her grandfather to get her out.

I didn't talk to my father about it for another couple of days. Grace was out on bail, staying with Dad at his house. I stopped by to see what I could learn.

Grace was terrifically unhappy. I could tell. She avoided me completely. She was dressed in sweatpants. She was swelling at the hips and abdomen. Her hair was greasy and pulled back in a pony tail. She had acne. She went in the guest bedroom and closed the door.

I asked Dad to take a ride with me.

We went outside, got in my car, and I drove. I asked what had happened.

"We got rid of the nigger," he said. "Thank God Almighty, we've gotten rid of him."

I pressed for more information. It had cost Dad a lot of money and a favor from well-connected legal counsel. Grace was out on bond and stood a very good chance of simply being charged with under-age possession of alcohol.

Bobby, on the other hand, was in serious trouble.

"The little boyfriend," Dad said, "is going to prison on drug charges. He's gone."

"But what about the child?" I blurted out. "What about his child?"

Dad just rode on in silence. He hadn't quite thought that through yet. Or if he had, he wasn't talking about it.

I never saw Bobby Lewson again. But I never see most of them again, the pants-sagging, young, African-American men I try so hard to save. They just disappear from class one day, and God knows where they fly off to.

Uncle Romulus

In the middle of the 1895 South Carolina Constitutional Convention, Robert Smalls was called away from his duties in Columbia to attend the Beaufort bedside of his ailing, beloved wife, Annie, nearly twenty years his junior.

And, while he was home, Annie died.

By the accounts we have, mostly family accounts, Robert was inconsolable.

We do not know what illness took Annie's life. She would be buried, after one of those shouting and wailing and stomping and dancing funerals, in an unmarked grave at the colored church over in what was getting to be that side of town.

She would just disappear, like those thug birds that fly away from my community college English classes. We'd be kidding ourselves if we imagined that this event, as central as it was to the life of our man Robert Smalls, was of any consequence at all in the course of the affairs of state of South Carolina or the United States of America.

There is a granite marker on Annie's grave now, as there is on Hannah's and on Robert's. But those granite markers are clearly of 20th-Century origin, as is the bronze bust of Robert Smalls marking the small churchyard and the eternal resting place of the King of Beaufort County, the High Lord of Niggerdom himself.

But here we are swirling about in the hatred that ruled that time and that ruled the century afterwards and that lurks, right beneath the surface, in our very own time, and that resides still, no matter how I try to purge it, in my very own being (why else would my fingers so nimbly type the word "nigger?"). We are forgetting the real truth of this episode, that there in the house on Prince Street, the house I have seen myself twice now in person, and pointed out lovingly to my wife, who found the place so beautiful, there in that house in the upstairs bedroom, the portly, gray, battered man, the man who had lived a life founded in love and decency and hope- only to be beaten down and crushed at every turn just because of the genetic variation that gave him darker skin and kinky hair- that this man, the man I have grown to love even though I never knew him, this man has thrown himself across the still-warm body of the love of his life. His young son stands beside him, sobbing, holding his grown sister's hand. The old man is sobbing. He is wailing, and as his heroic chest rises and falls, the bed and the corpse of his beloved quake beneath him.

For how much longer (you've been wondering, I know) will Robert Smalls have to wander before he goes home to be with Annie? What monsters and scheming gods and unworthy, slinking, scheming men will he have to face before he can find himself in the fullness of grace and be the hero he was made to be?

Robert Smalls wailed and came apart in that house, and after the passing of his Annie, according to family accounts, he slept in that same bedroom in that same bed with his young, half-orphaned son Willie for many years to come. He showed the boy, by all accounts, the same doting love Henry McKee had showed him in the same house a lifetime earlier, in another world- the same, decent love of the father that is in all of us, that every single one of us can summon at any moment and give to any other human being at any moment of any day, and that so very, very few of us ever put into action. Henry McKee, that utterly inconsequential, white, antebellum planter, had put that love into action for that young slave boy in his house. Maybe he had learned the love from the boy's mother, Lydia, his slave and nanny. Maybe Lydia had learned it from her mother, and that mother learned it from her grandmother, who learned it in the dark, pagan jungles of West Africa, from thousands of generations of vodu-wailing, wheel-dancing, devil-worshipers plotting to enslave their fellow Africans. But from somewhere, from somewhere out there beyond all these people, that love came, and it was given, and everything that was worthwhile, everything that makes this story worth telling, everything that makes our lives worth living, truly everything and the only thing that is important to any of us, all of that came from and through this love.

Everything. And Robert Smalls could do nothing now but let that love flow through him. Because everything else had been taken from him. Or it would be soon.

The Statesman

After all that stupid ruckus caused by Smalls's cohabiting-with-a-coon clause, we were on to the real task at hand, which was the establishment of decent, honorable government in this state led and controlled entirely by white men.

Now you can see the political genius of Ben Tillman. The timing was right. All across the South, all across the nation, people were beginning to realize what an enormous danger the colored race posed to this country. We couldn't get rid of them all. There were just too many, but we had to get them in a place where the white man could keep them under control. We had taken care of the Indians. There had been few enough that we could kill most of them. Now it was time to take care of the nigras.

Under the choreography of Ben Tillman we wrote a constitution that took the vote away from the colored man. Now, you might find a handful of obstinate niggers in this state who care so little for their lives or the lives of their families that they will still show up and cast a ballot on election day, but they are few and far between.

After all this had been worked through the various committees, and we were about ready to vote on it at the convention, that was when I understood why Ben Tillman had allowed Smalls and his handful of coloreds to be seated as delegates, for all the aggravation and trouble they caused. (They were even getting written up in the South Carolina papers as decent, eloquent statesmen who were standing up for the rights of the Negro.)

But Tillman was just letting Smalls run with the rope.

When everything was saucered and blowed and ready for a vote, that rascal Smalls stood up to give one more speech about the rights of the Negro and justice and democracy and whatever. Ben Tillman let him run on just like a Baptist preacher called by the spirit in the Sunday afternoon service. Smalls wore himself out and sat down.

Then Tillman rose to speak, and I understood. I was a young man, and I saw how politics really works. Ben Tillman lifted the sword effortlessly in his strong, rhetorical arm, and he swooped it down on Smalls's neck.

Ben spoke just as kindly and diplomatically as he could. He treated the old colored man with exaggerated respect, treated him as an elder statesman, an honored opponent, a worthy man, who was speaking for things we all believe in, and it just pained Ben terribly, it was something he absolutely hated to do, but he needed to remind the convention of the simple truth.

This man Smalls had been convicted of bribery, Ben reminded the world, when he was an elected member of the South Carolina Senate.

Smalls had been convicted by a jury of colored men, in an open and free trial. So how, Ben asked, how, could a man with that kind of record be trusted with the governance of a state in the American Union?

It was timed magnificently. I turned to watch Smalls as Ben was speaking. I saw the other colored men watching Smalls, too.

Something broke in Smalls as Ben spoke.

Smalls knew now why he had been resurrected and invited.

He was the main exhibit.

The other nigras, the ones that had been so proud of him for the past few weeks, understood then the role they, too, had been brought to play.

In politics, you see men defeated and broken. It comes so suddenly. It often comes subtly. It rarely comes when they are expecting it. But when the moment happens, when they realize all is lost, they can see it like the sun shining on an icy, January day.

Smalls stood to speak again. But he knew what had happened and how he had been used. He knew now the role he had been playing all along, the nigger to do his little dance for the grown-ups.

Smalls could be a dynamic speaker, but now he rambled. He spoke in circles. He... well it was sad to watch. It's sad to watch a man be defeated and finished in public, whether you're for him or against him.

Smalls sat down, silenced. Within a couple of days, he was gone from the convention. The excuse was that someone at home was sick. His wife or someone. I think he came back for a few days right at the end. He and the other few colored delegates refused to sign the final constitution we adopted, but by that time, it didn't matter. Ben Tillman had created the future.

The Wheelman

Robert Smalls' speech in response to Ben Tillman at the state constitutional convention, November 2, 1895:

Mr. President, I had thought that I would not find it necessary to have a word to say in regard to this contest for the right of freemen, for the question had been ably presented by others; but to my surprise I find the distinguished gentlemen from Edgefield, Mr. Tillman and Mr. J.C. Sheppard, going away from the all important question, the right to let free Americans cast an honest ballot for honest men.

By those Gentlemen I am arranged here and placed on trail for an act said to have been committed in 1873 in South Carolina. It is true, sir, that I was arrested in the state in 1877, charged by the Democrats of the state with receiving a bribe in 1873....

Now, let me say that after that trial and after I was arrested I appealed to the supreme court of the state. The supreme court held that opinion off over one year, as the record will show. After I had run for congress a second time the supreme court rendered a decision sustaining the action of the lower court. After that was done, under Section 641 of the Revised Statutes, I took an appeal to the Supreme Court of the United States. I went to Washington and appeared before that court. The record shows it, I went before Chief Justice Waite, and he granted the appeal and docketed the case.

No sooner was this done, and no sooner had I returned to South Carolina, than, without a single word from me, or friend of mine, directly or indirectly, Governor Simpson, of South Carolina, issued and sent to me in Beaufort a pardon, which I have here in this paper.

Why should this matter be dragged into this debate? Why, sir, it is to inflame the passions of delegates against Republicans and force them to vote for this most infamous Suffrage Bill, which seeks to take away the right to vote from two-thirds of the qualified voters of the state.

It has been claimed that there has been a compromise in my case, but this is not true. I refused all offers of compromise, but there were compromises made but I was not included; I received no advantage there from. I have here a copy of a compromise entered into by the state of South Carolina and the United States District Attorney for South Carolina, which I send to the desk and ask that it be read, which speaks for itself:

Mr. President, I am through with this matter. It should not have been brought in here. All the thieves are gone; they are scattered over this floor, and I shall serve them to the best of my ability.

My race needs no special defense, for the past history of them in this country proves them to be as good as any people anywhere. All they need is an equal chance in the battle of life. I am proud of them, and by their acts toward me I know that they are not ashamed of me, for they have at all times honored me with their votes.

I stand here the equal of any man. I started out in the war with the Confederates; they threatened to punish me and I left them. I went to the Union army. I fought in seventeen battles to make glorious and perpetuate the flag that some of you trampled under your feet.

Innocent of every charge attempted to be made here today against me, no act or word of yours can in any way blur the record that I have made at home and abroad.

Mr. President, I am through, and shall not hereafter notice any personal remark. You have the facts in the case; by them I ask to be judged.

Uncle Romulus

Grace disappeared from my parents' house about a week after Bobby Large's incarceration. There was a row. Very hurtful things were said. Bridges were burned.

I gathered this from my a phone conversation with my father.

And then she was gone. We didn't know where she was. My daughters, her cousins, didn't know where she was. She had scorched her bridge with Mary. Mary wasn't returning her calls. I found this out later. From Mary. It was a source of guilt in the months and years afterwards.

I found Grace serendipitously nearly a month later. I was in Charleston, visiting my in-laws. They told me they heard she had moved there. One of my wife's cousins had run into her. My in-laws were fishing for gossip. They wanted me to say Grace was pregnant.

They wanted me to say the father was black. They wanted me to say she was mentally ill. They wanted me to name the illness.

They already knew all this. Everyone they knew probably knew all this by now, in some variation on the truth created in the gossip cycle. But I knew the truth. I didn't want to participate in this exercise.

As soon as I got out of their house, I dialed Grace's cell number. It rang ten or so times. No answer. Went to voice mail. I hung up and redialed. Same thing.

Hung up and redialed, and this time she answered.

"Hey," she said.

"I'm in Charleston," I said.

A long, long silence.

"You want to talk?" I said.

A long, long silence. But she didn't hang up.

"I love you," I said.

"You have no idea," she said.

I was silent.

"I'll meet you down at Folly Beach," I said. "Down at the parking lot at the end of the road. Where the surfers park. We can go for a walk."

Another silence.

"What time?" she asked.

I looked at my watch. Only the travel time was relevant. Why did I look at my watch?

"Half an hour?" I said.

"O.k."

And that was it. I was driving. I crossed the James Island Connector bridge, driving over brown tidal river and the green marsh. I entertained fantasies of salvaging this situation. I prayed. I prayed and listened. I didn't like what I was hearing. I prayed to say the right thing. I prayed to do the right thing. I prayed to listen the right way. I didn't like what I was hearing.

It took me half an hour to drive to our meeting place. Lots of traffic lights.

Grace was already in the parking lot when I arrived. She was sitting in the driver's seat of her car, smoking a cigarette with the door open and her feet hanging out.

When I walked up, I could see she was in the bad place.

She snatched a heavy, bulging pocketbook from the passenger seat and got out of the car. "All right," she said. "Let's do this."

She stormed off down the trail leading from the parking lot toward Lighthouse Inlet.

I followed. She was walking fast, her pocketbook slung over her shoulder. With her other hand, she was tugging the pocketbook against her side as she walked. The effect was of someone twisting herself needlessly.

I followed at a distance of twenty or so feet, barely able to keep up, but not speaking.

After a few hundred yards, Grace turned and glared at me. I stopped.

"You wanted to talk," she said.

"Let's keep walking," I said. "It's pretty."

She glared.

"Have you ever been out there?" I asked.

Grace turned and walked. This time she walked beside me down the trail. It was a former road, now closed to traffic and sprouting weeds through the cracks. We soon emerged to the beach alongside the inlet. Surf was breaking on the inlet bar to our right.

Morris Island was a few hundred yards across the inlet to our left. Straight ahead, standing in the ocean, was an abandoned lighthouse. Beach erosion had left it stranded a half mile from the nearest land.

I led Grace along the beach, which stretched away ahead of us, deserted. Sand dunes lay now to our left. The inlet lay to our right. Behind the sand dunes lay nothing but marsh and creeks running all the way back to James Island in the far distance.

This was, you will note, the location where Robert Smalls became the first black captain in U.S. Naval history.

I didn't know who Robert Smalls was at the time.

I wanted to hold on to Grace, and Grace was slipping away. I knew it.

We talked as we walked. She still walked furiously, tugging on her bag with one hand, and twisting herself with the effort. She talked in mad circles tangentially related to actual events.

Her talk was related to Bobby Lewson. It was related to his incarceration. It was related to her pregnancy. It was related to her educational disasters. It was related to her chaotic employment history. It was related to her co-dependent, constantly-intervening family. It was related to her drug use. It was related to the sight of her mother, who, when Grace found her, had the top of her skull removed by a shotgun blast. The shotgun muzzle had been applied at the roof of her mouth. By Grace's report, given to my daughters within my earshot, the result was the most bizarre distortion of face and features. The top of the head was blown upwards and apart like a burst watermelon, but with loose folds of skin and hair draped over the exploded gore. Only minutes before, this was her mother. Just before she sent Grace up to the corner store to buy some milk. Only minutes before in a state like Grace.

All of Grace's talk was related to reality, but it seemed so removed from reality. So completely disjointed. How could one take the facts and twist them to this conclusion? How could one reach these interpretations? They seemed so disconnected, but they streamed forth as naturally as the sea breeze was building little whitecaps on the ebbing stream of the inlet, blowing streams of white sand along the gray beach, stinging our ankles as we walked.

"Why don't you admit it, Uncle Rom?" she said. "Why don't you admit it? You hate him, too. You all hate him. To you, he's just a nigger. That's all. That's all you can really see, and you hate him for it."

I just listened.

"And now I've got a little one inside of me, and it's more than you can stand. It's more than all of you can stand. They're talking about it, aren't they? They're talking about me. I'm crazy. Her mother killed herself. She's been living with that nigger boy, and now she's got a little one inside her. They're talking about it all over, aren't they?"

I just listened. I didn't say anything.

"I want you to tell me something, Uncle Rom All this crap you've been telling me all my life, all this crap about love, and grace, and the arc of the moral fucking universe, and God loves you, and you love me, and all that fucking crap, it's just crap, isn't it? It's just a bunch of crap you made up, because it makes you feel better, and it makes you forget how hateful a person you really are, and how you're not really like that at all, and how the whole goddamn universe isn't like that at all. That's the way it really is, isn't it? And you don't want to admit that to me, do you?"

This brought silence.

"Well," she said. "I'm just going to fix it. I'm going to solve everybody's goddamned problem."

She reached into her bag, and she pulled out Bobby Large's Glock.

She put the muzzle up to the side of her head, and, before I could reach her, she turned to face the inlet and pulled the trigger.

Pink foam sprayed across my face.

A scarlet fountain of blood gushed forth.

And her body dropped to the beach in front of me.

And there. I told it. I didn't know if I could.

Uncle Romulus

That much I can recall. My mind is trying to erase it, but it can't.

When Grace's mother killed herself, a relative proposed Grace receive an experimental medical treatment that was being tested on soldiers in the Iraqi war. Drugs could be administered within the first thirty days of the witnessed traumatic event, so the memory could be sufficiently clouded, and Post Traumatic Stress syndrome could be avoided.

We didn't do it to Grace. We should have.

I've often wished I could do it. I can't forget what I just told you.

My mind has successfully forgotten much of what went on after Grace's suicide. I vaguely remember being on the beach, holding her body. I remember screaming.

I remember how much the screaming hurt my throat. I remember feeling as if the top of my head would pop off from my screams.

I remember people coming. Eventually.

I remember the police. I remember questioning. I was a suspect. They questioned me thoroughly and carefully, for a long time. I cannot remember the details of the conversation. For some reason or the other, the police pretty quickly let me go.

Go where? God, I don't even want to try to remember any more. I don't want to try to remember. I remembered that fucking day for you. Isn't that enough?

I bought the first sailboat sometime after Grace died. I do remember that. If I think back on it, that was probably within a year of when I lost my business and had to be hospitalized for suicidal ideations, probably in the same year I went broke, and my wife left, and my wife came back, and I got the teaching job. Oh, I'm jumbling all that up. I can't really remember it in order, now. If somebody would put a time line on the Internet, like they have for Robert Smalls's life, I could probably put it in some order. But I really don't want to go back there. I went back to part of it for you. That's all I want to go back for. Can't you just let me be?

Why can't we just let each other be? Why can't they let Robert Smalls be? Why does he have to be a saint? Why does he have to be the Martin Luther King, Jr., of his century? Why must we build a monument? Why must he be made into some grotesque parody of a man- something like Wade Hampton and Ben Tillman, frozen larger than life on the statehouse grounds? Can't he just be like I am? Like Grace was? Can't he just be? Isn't that enough? You make a story or a myth out of it, if you want to. I've had enough.

Marshall Evans

The Southern Paper

Charleston News and Courier, November 4, 1895 (the day before Annie Smalls died):

No one can fail to be impressed with Gen. Smalls' earnest protestation, before God, of his innocence of the charge of bribe-taking of which he was convicted in 1877. He alone knows whether he was justly convicted or not, but we think it is due to him to recall the public knowledge of the fact that he demanded a trial when he could easily have kept out of the way, and when white men who were under accusations of wrong-doing with him fled the State.

It is the simple statement of a fact to say that he was tried at a time and under circumstances that did not tend to insure him of a fair trial, and that not a few white men in Columbia who attended his trial held the evidence offered to be insufficient to convict him. The action of the jury has been subject to criticism and remark in Columbia from that day to this, and we believe it safe to say that he could not be convicted before a jury of impartial white men anywhere on the same evidence today. Perhaps some of the lawyers or citizens of Columbia will take the trouble to correct or confirm what we have said in the interest of justice.

In the next several decades, no Columbia lawyer or citizen actually took the trouble to confirm what the News and Courier said here.

Uncle Romulus

Robert Smalls lived in Beaufort for another twenty years after the Constitutional Convention of 1895. Twenty years is a very long time in a man's life. Twenty years is enough time for your entire outlook to change, for your family to change in its makeup and status. It is enough time for the society in which you live to be transformed, utterly. To skip over twenty years of a man's life in a few pages is to perform the most obscene omission in one's duty as a storyteller, but all biographers of Smalls do so. They are interested in Smalls the public man. But I am only interested in Smalls the private man, now. Smalls the public man is someone you build a monument to. Now I only care about the man Smalls really was.

In 1900, Smalls still enjoyed a small measure of political influence. In that year, Congress awarded him another five thousand dollars in prize money for the capture of the *Planter*. Smalls had been trying for decades to collect more money from the Federal government for that feat. I don't know how to put that effort into perspective, honestly.

It doesn't strike me as noble.

It sounds like something I would do.

Smalls was the Customs Collector of Beaufort until 1911, when the Democratic Senators from South Carolina managed to wrest that federal job from him. Near the end of his tenure as Customs Collector, Smalls lost his foot to diabetes. He had to walk on crutches for the rest of his life. Or he sat, fat and aged, in his chair.

By 1912, Smalls had become ornery and disagreeable, quick to anger and quick to take offense, according to his youngest son Willy (interviewed in the mid-20th Century). Robert spent most of his time sitting on the front porch of his home on Prince Street, a bitter old man.

This seems to me to be the early stages of Alzheimer's, which I (and you) have seen in so many people we have known and loved. I see it now in my father. Whenever we get together, he comes back around to the missing link in our family tree, the one I have become convinced is a black man. He speaks in confused but earnest circles against that theory. He says if he could only go to Charleston and find the right record in the right location he could establish the entire line of our family tree, unbroken, with its rightful forbears in the right places. But he will not go there. He will not remember the issue much longer. In all likelihood he will pass into oblivion long before he passes into oblivion. The overwhelming odds are, I will soon follow him.

When Robert Smalls died in 1915, the First World War was well into its first year. Most white-oriented newspapers, even in Beaufort, South Carolina, did not even note his passing. The Charleston *News and Courier* posted only a brief notice, giving Smalls's title as "General", but saying nothing about his life.

According to historical accounts, the Adams Street Band played at Smalls's funeral in Beaufort. In the funeral procession leading up to the church, they honored their tradition of playing slow, doleful music. The King of Beaufort County was interred between his two wives, next to the clapboard sanctuary of the Tabernacle Baptist Church.

When the funeral service ended, the Adams Street Band burst into a joyous, raucous celebration, as was their custom, and the entire gathering danced away through the streets of Beaufort.

As that music boomed out, I wonder what birds started from the live oaks overhead, spreading their wings and flying off toward the river and the far horizon.

Uncle Romulus

Late in the summer of 2013, my wife took a week of vacation. She and I sailed to Beaufort, South Carolina. We spent our first night at anchor in Steamboat Creek on John's Island. That evening, after we had eaten supper, dolphins began to gather where we were anchored. They surfaced and blew peacefully around us in the waning daylight. Occasionally one would lift its tail from the water and slap the water's surface. A couple of times a dolphin jumped clear of the water to look us over.

Some dolphins would swim slowly and gently in pairs or threes near the surface, touching each other. It was the most beautiful and peaceful of settings. It was like a sojourn on C. S. Lewis's planet Perelandra, a paradise that had never fallen, where evil was a thing that reigned far away- on the distant planet Earth, the silent planet.

The next morning we rose early and motored south on the Intracoastal Waterway. When we got to Beaufort in the early afternoon, we decided to stay a night or two in the municipal marina, half a block off Front Street, where over a century before Robert Smalls paraded with the Adams Street Band and called out Wade Hampton as a fraud. My wife and I walked up to the marina office to register. We learned we had arrived in the middle of the Beaufort Water Festival, a week-long celebration. That night was Motown Night, with live music in the waterfront park that runs along the river near the marina.

As evening came, we grilled steaks on our boat and had dinner watching the sun set over the bluffs south of town. The bluffs were lined with elegant houses set back in the live oaks.

After supper, we walked up to the park for Motown Night.

I'm not sure where Robert Smalls' Customs House office would have been. Would it have been on Front Street, with the back of the building looking over this waterfront?

That evening there was a huge stage erected. The lawn in front of the stage, underneath the live oaks and Spanish moss, was filled with several hundred people listening to Motown tunes and a band from Savannah. The crowd was white people and black people all mixed together. There was no self-consciousness visible. As the band broke into a song by the Four Tops, two African-American women walking beside us shouted in jubilation and began to dance.

My wife leaned to me and said, "I didn't know black people liked this music."

I was silent.

The band sang and played, and the humid, summer night grew darker and cooler. My wife and I wandered from one end of the park to the other. People of all ages and of all races, but mostly black or white (as Americans know black and white), danced and clapped and rejoiced at tunes they had known for a lifetime. Elderly black women swayed to the music, as animated as teenagers. A white man my age played and danced with a mulatto toddler. He kissed and hugged her.

As I walked and danced and held my wife's hand for two or three hours in this scene, I grew increasingly emotional. I have shared with you now the story of the King of Beaufort County, his ultimate defeat and the decades of violence and injustice that followed. Yet this scene as devoid of evil as our interlude with the dolphins the night before in Steamboat Creek.

My wife was dancing more than I could keep up. I had to step aside. It was getting dark. She didn't notice me wiping my eyes.

I'm not making this up, now.

The lead singer, having worked the crowd up to that point where so many are willing to participate, asked the dancers in front of the stage to space themselves carefully for a special dance. He asked the people around them to give the dancers more room.

The band played a song called *The Cupid Shuffle* (I have since learned.) It is a zydeco/rap song.

In *The Cupid Shuffle*, a refrain directs the dancers "to the left, to the left, to the right, to the right, now kick, now kick, now walk it by yourself." Two- to three-hundred dancers in the audience began moving in unison. They all shuffled to the left, then they shuffled to the right, then they kicked and they kicked, then they danced their little dance.

My wife jumped in with them. The singer was a black man. The crowd was about half black and half white, and all were transported by joy, dancing in the most peaceful and the most amazing unison.

They all spun when they were supposed to spin. Then they joined in their choreographed sidestepping. It looked like a Bollywood director had been drilling them for days in preparation for this scene. This scene occurred in the Riverfront Park in Beaufort, South Carolina on the evening of July 22, 2013.

Really, I'm not making it up.

Perhaps you were there, and you remember it.

A few days later, near the end of my wife's vacation, we were sailing offshore back to Charleston. As we passed the north end of Folly Island, the Morris Island light came into view. My wife asked me where we were. I told her that was Lighthouse Inlet.

This brought silence.

I began to cry. I tried to stop it. But it wouldn't stop. I began to sob, and then I began to quake with the sobbing. My wife came to my side of the cockpit. She sat beside me and held me in her arms. She held me for a long, long time, and the autopilot took us on toward Charleston.

Our autopilot has a bit of a flaw. When you have the mainsail trimmed too tight, and there is weather helm in the boat, the belt will slip ever so slightly around the pulley on the steering wheel over time. You can't notice it slipping, but the boat's heading changes over time. You can see the track that has been traced on the chartplotter is a gently bending arc, rather than a straight line.

When I regained my composure an hour or two later, and I went below to check our course, I found the arc had led us toward the vestigial Charleston Harbor channel of Robert Smalls's time, the channel through which he piloted the *Keokuk* to attack the Holy City in that futile gesture of war.

I had to adjust our course to starboard to sail into the modern entrance, between the two long jetties.

We sailed into Charleston Harbor that afternoon. My wife wanted to sail as close as possible to Fort Sumter. We tacked to within a hundred yards or so of the fort, right where Robert Smalls steamed past in the *Planter* in his famous flight to freedom, as close as he may have come later in the *Keokuk*. Fort Sumter is still there, in the same spot, but it is two stories shorter than it was when Smalls steamed past. In the weeks after Union troops captured Morris Island, Federal artillery blew off the top two stories

That's all I have to tell you, I think, about the arc of the moral universe.

Uncle Romulus

As for me, I am what I am. I live now, paradoxically, maintained by a sense of anticipation. I anticipate a reality that I do not know is real. This may well be self-delusion. But it doesn't feel like delusion.

You may remember my discussion with Grace in the shadow of Wade Hampton. Grace spoke of the Ghent altar piece and its central motif, "The Adoration of the Mystic Lamb."

That image at the center of the Ghent altar piece was burned into my imagination nearly three decades ago, when I stood in front of the multi-paneled painting at the Ghent Cathedral.

I look for the image on the Internet, and there I find it. There, in the middle panel of the altar piece, is "The Adoration of the Mystic Lamb. "

It is difficult to appreciate the impact of this central panel by looking at it on the Internet. You can't quite get close enough.

Maybe you can get some feel for what I'm talking about when you do your Google search. You may see a link to a National Public Radio story calling this "The Most Coveted Work of Art in the World."

Or maybe you'll see *The New York Times* article calling it "one of the most revered pictures in Western art history."

Keep searching. You may even discover the Ghent Altar Piece is the most stolen work of art in human history. Stolen, lost, found, restored to its rightful place- again, and again, and again- century after century after century.

Hitler and Goering nabbed it and hid it in a salt mine. The Allies sought it feverishly, returning it after the war to its rightful place in the cathedral.

But why?

Because, perhaps, it is the Lamb in the central panel that is so stunning. It is the Lamb, standing on a stone altar of sacrifice.

What captures us is his ineffable might and serenity, and the expression on his face.

Can you find a web site where you can zoom in enough to see the expression? There, when you zoom in, you may see He is staring at you. He is looking directly into your soul.

It is the same gaze and expression I find in photographs of the mature Robert Smalls.

Look again.

I think you also may find him there.

Now that I have recovered, in some small way, from watching Grace kill herself, I live in constant anticipation, in anticipation of that time, which will come very soon, I hope, when I can join in the perpetual adoration of the Lamb, alongside Grace and Robert Smalls and the countless others.

There at the focus of our eternity, beyond time and arcs, beyond evil and suffering, beyond justice and injustice, will stand the Lamb. He will stare into our souls. And a bright fountain of blood will pour from his breast into the golden grail of mystery.

I have seen this. I think it is true.

The End

Acknowledgements

Many thanks to those whose feedback on earlier drafts of this novel were of immeasurable help, especially Alan Tessaro, John Cribb, Ann Evans, Mary Mac Evans, Hank Steinberg, Betsy Teter, and David MacMahan. Thanks to Fayssoux Evans for the cover design and to Betsy Teter, Anne Waters, Kathie Bennett, Kel Landis, and John Cribb for publication advice.

Thank you Dr. David Cox for your help in surviving suicide.

We all owe a great deal to Dr. Helen Boulware Moore and Michael Boulware Moore for their work in telling the world about their ancestor, Robert Smalls. Four biographers of Smalls- Dorothy Sterling, Okon Edet Uya, Edward A. Miller, and especially Andrew Billingsley, provided much of the historical material that made this wild fictionalization possible, although one wonders if they would be glad to know they had a part in it. And I owe a debt of gratitude to the staffs of the Kennedy Room at Spartanburg County Library, the South Carolina State Museum, and the U.S. Library of Congress for their help in locating hard-to-find documents about Robert Smalls.

If any doubt remains, at the end of this voyage of discovery, I found myself holding Smalls in the very highest reverence.

About the Author: Marshall Evans has worked as a peach farmer, international businessman, hedge fund manager, advisor to a governor, and English professor. He is the author of *Ten Tales of Improbable Escape Stolen from the Thief Giovanni Boccaccio*. He and his wife currently live in South Carolina and go sailing whenever they can.

Made in United States
Orlando, FL
20 September 2023